Some secrets won't stay buried.

ISLE of EVER

NEW YORK TIMES BESTSELLING AUTHOR

JEN CALONITA

ISLE OF EVER

JEN CALONITA

sourcebooks
young readers

Published by Sourcebooks Young Readers, an imprint of Sourcebooks Kids
P.O. Box 4410, Naperville, Illinois 60567-4410
(630) 961-3900
sourcebookskids.com

Cataloging-in-Publication Data is on file with the Library of Congress.

This product conforms to all applicable CPSC and CPSIA standards.

Source of Production: Maple Press, York, Pennsylvania, USA
Date of Production: December 2024
Run Number: 5033473

Printed and bound in the United States of America.
MA 10 9 8 7 6 5 4 3 2 1

For my grandparents, Nicholas and Kathleen Calonita,
who taught me to search for buried treasures

Some secrets won't stay buried.

PROLOGUE

ENTRY 1

From Evelyn Terry's Private Journal,
Dated June 4, 1825

> The tide brought in many
> things, but this was the
> first time it brought a person...

"Race you to the island, Sparrow!" Gilbert Monroe shouted as he ran ahead of me down the wet path, sand and dirt kicking up behind him. Rain was still misting after the storm. "I'm going to beat you!"

"No, you're not!" I ran faster, thundering down the rocky

path, laughing as the bucket I carried for shells banged against my bare legs. I could hear the others behind us—Aggy, Thomas, and Laurel, taking bets on who would be victorious in making it to our island first.

It would be me. It is always me.

I rounded the bend at the bottom of the hill where overgrown brush hid our island from view, and I crashed into Gilbert. We both tumbled to the ground.

"Are you alright?" Gil asked, immediately helping me up. Mud crusted the bottom of my dress and stained both of Gil's knees. He even had a splotch of it on his cheek. My bare feet were caked in dirt. "I didn't mean to stop short and get in your way. I was waiting for you to catch up."

I narrowed my eyes suspiciously. "Catch up?" I jutted out my chin defiantly. "I don't need your help to win a race. I can do that on my own."

"Oh, I know." Gil brushed his pale brown hair away from his big hazel eyes. "You're the best at everything, Sparrow." His cheeks warmed and he quickly looked away.

My friends call me Sparrow because I am sharp-eyed, nimble, and quick, like the bird that dots the Long Island shoreline we call home.

"I don't know about *that*," I teased. "But I am fast." We both grinned.

Even though Gilbert is fourteen and two years older than me, we've been in the same class for three years now, since he came from England to live with his aunt and uncle after his parents died from typhoid fever. They run the mercantile in town for Axel Rudd's father and live in rooms above the shop. I was glad Axel didn't come with us tonight. He's rude. We try to leave him out when we can, but it is tough avoiding him.

Another rumble of thunder in the distance made us look up. The sky was darkening both from the vicious rain and wind that had just passed and the approaching twilight. The clouds still looked heavy and thick, ominous as if more rain was imminent. The roads and the fields were already flooded. Trees were bent and snapped at odd angles. *Please don't rain again*, I thought. *Just hold off for an hour more so we can go to the island.* We were so close now. Once we cut through the brush, and the seagrass, we'd be on the beach, and then the small island I found would be in view. I wasn't sure why, but every time I emerged onto the beach, the sandbar was there, waiting as if it knew I was coming. I wanted to see our island again so badly. If we didn't make it there today, between chores and school, it could be a week before we could meet up here again. I didn't want to wait a week to see Gil and the friends I loved most in this world.

"How did you get away today?" Gil asked.

"My mother thinks I'm out checking on our grapevines," I admitted sheepishly.

A merchant from Italy gave Papa a single grapevine. Mama didn't want him to plant the vine. She didn't think it would take, but it did. And so far, the vines are growing, winding, and creeping along, getting bigger by the year.

"My aunt and uncle think I'm making a delivery, but I finished all the mercantile deliveries before supper." Gil grinned.

He had a large freckle on the left side of his mouth and a sprinkling of them across the bridge of his nose that grew brighter in the sun, which he tries to avoid by always wearing a large hat. My heart did a strange sort of thump as I stared at him for a moment.

Having a fondness for Gil is my secret.

"We only told a small fib and for a very good reason," I said. "When we're on the island, I feel like it's our time, and I can actually...breathe."

I looked out at the small parcel of land—our island—that we claimed as our own only a few weeks ago. This small stretch of land that jutted out from Greenport, where we lived, was hidden by brush and overgrowth along the water as if it never wanted to be found. But when we did a few weeks ago, we couldn't stop returning to it again and again. The island felt like its own place, so unlike the rest of Greenport. Where else could one find strange giant conch shells that felt like they'd washed up from halfway across the world? A waterfall, where we swam, ever mindful of the cave behind it that we were all too chickenhearted to explore? The sand on our island is warm, the sun always seems brighter, and sometimes—though I've never shared this—it feels like the wind off the water whispers my name over and over again when I am there. *Evelyn. Evelyn Terry. Welcome home.*

"Me too. And we found this place thanks to you," Gil reminded me. "Maybe that's why I always think of it as 'Evelyn Island.'"

The two of us were quiet and I looked away quickly so he couldn't see me blush. That's when I heard the others coming.

"Who won?" asked Thomas as he came down the road with Laurel, the girl he was courting, by his side. Thomas and Laurel are older than the rest of us—sixteen—and I suspect they won't stay in Greenport once they were married. Both want to see the world. My best friend, Aggy, quiet, always serious and kind, trailed behind them, her curly brown hair flying behind her, her gray eyes standing out on her pale face. She looked from me to Gil back to me again.

"It was a tie," Gil said and winked at me.

"It was only a tie if Sparrow let you win," Laurel said, and we all laughed.

"It doesn't matter who won," I said. "I just want to get to

the island. I bet we're going to find the most magnificent shells after tonight's storm."

Lightning flashed in the distance, and we all looked up. A low rumble of thunder made me doubt that the storm really was finished. I thought of Papa's tide clock, and I knew that high tide would return before we knew it. If we wanted time on the island and didn't want to get trapped there, we had to go now.

"New race?" asked Thomas, his tone daring. "Whoever gets to the sandbar first keeps all the shells! Go!"

We all took off running down the path, pushing away the brush that hid the shoreline to burst through it and race over the sandbar to the island. Even in the dark, I could already see the island in my mind's eye—warm, sunny, like it always is—calling to me again. I picked up speed and ran ahead of everyone, even Thomas, who I suspected was hanging back so he could hold Laurel's hand. I could hear Aggy and Gil on my heels, but I was first, running so hard my legs were burning, my lungs screaming.

There was a loud clap of thunder. It rattled me, sounding like a thousand trees falling at once, and then suddenly a man was standing in front of me on the sandbar. He had his hands on his hips, and looked perturbed to see me.

"Where do you think you're going, kid?"

His eyes were hard to pull away from. Azure blue, with flecks of gray that seemed to sparkle, they held my gaze. He was an adult, but much younger than my father, a smirk etched into his face.

"To the island," I said, pointing to the stretch of land emerging from the fog behind him, as if just coming into view. I could hear it calling to me. *Evelyn. Evelyn Terry. Welcome!*

"Ahhh. It's caught you in its clutches too then, has it?" He looked back at the island, then to me again. "Let me save you some heartache, kid." He was impossibly tall, and when he leaned into whisper in my ear, the scruff of his blond beard tickled my face. "Run from this island and don't look back."

I looked at him then—really looked—and for some reason, it didn't occur to me that the others hadn't reached the sandbar yet. I didn't wonder how this oddly dressed man had appeared out of nowhere. He wore a long leather coat, a matching vest worn over a threadbare white shirt, rings on his fingers, and an earring in his left ear. A key with a skull insignia hung from a chain around his neck. He had a gold compass in his hands. He stared at it a moment, then snapped its cover shut.

"Who are you?" I whispered. It was a simple question, but it would have the most complicated answer I'd ever hear.

His smirk deepened. "You wouldn't believe me if I told you."

My heart thudded in my chest. "I might. Try me."

He scratched his head, his floppy blond hair blowing in the wind. "Alright then. Ever heard of the name Kimble? Captain Jonas Kimble?"

I blinked. "No."

He looked a bit affronted. "No? How can that be?" he said, sounding exasperated. "Don't they teach you kids any—" He sighed heavily and checked the compass again. "No matter. What year is it, kid?"

"You mean day?" I asked, confused. "Today is June fourth."

"*When*?" he asked, his voice gruffer. "June fourth, *when*?"

"June fourth, eighteen twenty-five," I said.

He seemed to stumble back then. "Eighteen twenty-five... How?" His face flickered with pain, and he consulted the compass again. "I've wasted so much time."

Maybe he is lost, I reasoned. "Do you need directions to Greenport?" I asked, motioning to his compass.

His smile was almost teasing. "Who says I'm using this compass to find a port? Let me tell you something, kid. Sometimes the journey is more important than the final destination." He slipped the compass into his pocket.

I felt a hand on my shoulder and jumped.

"Sparrow, it's time to go," Aggy said, her eyes darting to the man then back to me. I could hear the worry in her voice.

Behind me I could hear Gil and the others calling me now too. And in the distance, another rumble of thunder.

"Now," said Aggy, more insistently.

"Listen to your friend," the man said, his eyes on the sky. "The Blood Orange Moon is coming, and you don't want to be here when it arrives."

"What is a Blood Orange Moon?" I asked as Aggy tugged on my arm.

"Sparrow, let's go!"

"You heard her," he said, watching us. "I've got no time to talk to kids. Now, if you knew where my ship was, that would be a different story." He scanned the horizon line.

"We don't know where it is," Aggy answered for us. "Good day, sir." She took my arm and led me away in a hurry.

"Aggy, why are you being rude?" I said, but she shushed me as we approached Thomas, Laurel, and Gil.

"Are you alright?" Laurel asked. "This fog rolled in out of nowhere, and we couldn't find our way to the sandbar."

"We thought maybe you fell in the water," Thomas said.

"No, I was just talking to—that man." I turned around. The man was gone. Aggy gave me a strange look.

"There's no man there," Laurel said.

"Sparrow? Are you alright?" Gil asked.

"Yes, there was a man on the sandbar. Just a moment ago," I said. "Aggy saw him. He was looking for his ship."

"Ship?" Thomas stared out at what we could see of the water. A flash of lightning lit up the sky again. "There's no ship in the harbor."

"Maybe he was sick with fever," Laurel suggested. "No fisherman would be out in this weather."

"Perhaps," I said, feeling odd. Aggy remained silent behind me.

The wind picked up then, and I knew it was the precursor to more rain.

"Let's go home," Thomas said. "We can't make it to the island before another storm. We'll try for shells again next week." He turned back the way we'd come, and Laurel and Gil followed. Aggy, however, stood still, staring out at the water shrouded in fog.

I looked too, and as the fog suddenly lifted, I knew we were seeing the same thing.

A battered ship, with a black flag bearing a skull and crossbones whipping in the wind, clear as day.

ONE

BENNY

BOSTON, PRESENT DAY

At the diner, Sal leaned out from the kitchen window to get a better look at the TV over the counter. "I'm telling you—the reality star looking to start his own production company is the murderer."

"You're wrong," said Benny, narrowing her brown eyes at the screen. Their new favorite show, *Lawyered Up*, was on. "I'm going with the skittish tutor with the college loans."

"The reality star had loans too," Sal insisted.

"Sal, table seven is still waiting on those onion rings," called one of the waitresses as she slapped another order ticket on the counter. "Hey, Benny! Heard it was your birthday last week! Twelve, right? Happy birthday!"

"Thanks, Carol," Benny said, remembering what she knew about the older waitress—semiretired, widowed, two adult kids who lived out of state. Sizing up people quickly was one of Benny's skills, something she'd learned from moving to new towns and changing schools so often.

"Onion rings are still frying," Sal grumbled. "Tell them if they wanted fast food, they could have gone to McDonald's."

Carol rolled her eyes at Benny as she grabbed two Greek salads from the window. "Why are you hanging out with this crank? Shouldn't you be out with friends?"

What friends? Benny thought. The ones she made slipped away every time they moved. As soon as the school year ended three weeks ago, they'd moved again, this time to Boston. It didn't help that Mom could afford only a single phone for the two of them. Who wanted to text someone whose mom could be reading their messages? "Sal is helping me celebrate," Benny told Carol. "Plus, I get free onion rings every time he gets the murderer wrong on *Lawyered Up.*"

"Not every time!" Sal said as he pulled the onion rings from the deep fryer, then turned and handed Carol a hamburger platter.

"That burger smells good," Benny said. "How about a game of rock, paper, scissors? If I win, you let me have a plate." At home, they'd run out of milk again, so all she'd had for breakfast was dry cereal. Not that she'd been too hungry at the time. Their new apartment over the Apollo Diner had no air-conditioning, so she avoided it as much as she could. She hung out in the diner during her mom's shifts, since it had free air, free cable, and, occasionally, free food.

Sal wiped the sweat from his bald brown head. "When I play you at that game, I always lose. How about this: If I'm right about the murderer, you get a burger. I'm wrong, you help me wash dishes."

"Deal." Benny didn't like to lose, but if she did, she could handle a few dishes. She'd had worse company than Sal before. Sal—tall, thin, bald, lived alone two blocks over, acted tough but had a cat he showed off pictures of like it was his kid, obsessed with *Law and Order*–type shows, like *Lawyered Up*. The best part about Sal? He wasn't trying to date her mom. "Sadly, you're going down."

Sal grabbed the remote to turn up the TV volume. "They're about to reveal who did it!"

Benny leaned forward, careful not to mess up the Scrabble board she had going with Mom, who'd take her turns whenever she passed by to grab her food orders from the kitchen.

"Brian Sullivan, you're under arrest for the murder of Sandra Milensky."

"YES!" Benny crowed as Sal slammed his spatula on the griddle. "Burger, please!"

Sal was already sliding the plate through the service window. "It's a bit overcooked."

"I'm not picky." She preferred her burgers well-done anyway. (Her mom suspected she might be a vegetarian who just hadn't committed to the lifestyle yet.) "I'll play you for a milkshake to go with it. Are you sure you aren't up for a round of rock, paper, scissors?"

Sal growled as he put another frozen patty on the grill. "No way. You got breakfast, lunch, *and* dinner out of me that way yesterday."

Benny smiled. Sal would cave. Her mom had only been working at the diner a few weeks, but Benny already had his number. There were worse ways to spend a summer afternoon. Still there was a part of her that wondered when her real life was going to start. Was Boston the place where that would finally happen? Twelve felt like a good year for life to begin.

"Stop eating the profits, Benny," said Mom, dropping off a ticket and picking up the special in the window. (Meatloaf. Benny wasn't a fan.) "I need this job."

"Hey, Sal made a bet. Your Scrabble move, by the way."

Mom turned the board so she could read it better. Benny couldn't help but think how pretty her mom was, despite the purple rings under her eyes from working double shifts. Her smile, her laugh, brown eyes, and naturally wavy brown hair that looked equally good in a ball cap or hanging over her eyes. Her mom swore Benny had the same hair and eyes, but Benny did not think she'd ever look like her. "Y-O-U-R," Mom said. "That's seven points. Top that."

Benny spun the small plastic travel board back toward her and studied her own letters. The Z she'd held on to for several rounds was proving problematic. No B meant the word zebra was out. But she did have an E and a P on the board. What about the R? Could she use that? She drummed her fingers on the counter. "How much time do I have?" Benny was patient. *Don't let them rush you. Take your time*, she heard Grams say. Grams taught her how to play Scrabble when she was five.

Her mom frowned. "I was supposed to get off at six, but Sal asked if I could pull another double, and we could use the cash."

Benny felt the hairs on her neck stand up. "How short are we?"

"I didn't say we were short." Her mom yanked at her black Apollo Diner tee. It had a picture of the Greek god on the front along with the words, *Everything's betta with a little feta*. "But..."

Benny groaned. "Tell me you didn't go back and buy that blue top at the thrift store!" She noticed Sal leaning in to listen, and she lowered her voice.

"It was on clearance," Mom protested. "And I have that date with Richard on Friday."

"*Richard*," Benny repeated, the name sticking on her tongue like taffy. "Who goes by *Richard* anymore? He sounds stuffy and pompous." *Pompous* was a good word. Worth thirteen points.

"He also drives a Tesla and owns two brownstones in Boston," Mom noted. "He could be good for us."

"We don't need anyone but each other," Benny reminded her, trying to stay calm. Her dad wasn't in the picture—Benny had never even met him—and the guys her mom dated always turned out to be cow dung. *Love doesn't work out for the women in our family*, Benny recalled Mom once telling her. Benny's grandmother had become a widow when she was pregnant with Mom and raised her alone. Grams had lived with Benny and her mom until she died two years ago. She had been a realist, like Benny. Mom, though, was still a romantic. Benny wished she'd realize, the only person they could rely on was each other.

"This Richard guy isn't going to save us," Benny continued. "Or pay our rent."

"I know, I know," Mom said, sounding worried now. "But I'll be honest: even if I return the top, we're still short for this week."

"Mom!" Benny scolded. "We counted the money the other night. We were so close."

"I couldn't get you nothing for your twelfth birthday," Mom insisted. "It's been such a rough year. You deserved that camera."

A Nikon F3 35mm camera. Benny had wanted an old camera like it forever. She liked to hear the sound of the click as she snapped a photo, the thrill of taking a picture and not knowing how it would look till she got the film developed. She sighed. "I love the Nikon. But maybe we should sell it."

"Benny," her mom groaned. "I'll stall on rent. I've done it before." She filled three glasses from the soda machine, placed them on a tray, and hurried off to serve them.

"Bad news" Sal obviously had been eavesdropping. "The landlord of this building always collects on the first...and if you don't have it, you're out of here."

Benny felt her insides twist. "Maybe we can reason with him."

Sal waved his spatula in the air. "I hate to be blunt, but you won't. Heck, I've rented this spot for ten years, and some months when business is slow, I think of flooding this place and collecting the insurance money." He raised an eyebrow. "The landlord does not negotiate on rent."

Benny turned back to her Scrabble board again, trying to calm her nerves. Then she placed *Z, Y, H*.

Sal leaned over the kitchen window. "That's not a word."

"*Zephyr* means *gentle breeze*. I just scored twenty-three

points." At least one thing was going her way today. She gave her swivel stool a spin and turned around just in time to see a man in an expensive suit approach the counter.

Sal looked at him. "Need a table?"

Benny stared at the man. In addition to the suit, he wore wire-rimmed glasses and a New York Yankees ball cap. She resisted the urge to reach for her new camera and take a picture of him.

"Actually, I'm looking for someone who I believe rents the apartment above this diner."

Benny's heart seized. Was this the landlord? She started to panic, her stomach swaying like she was on a ferry. "That's my mom."

He looked at her. "I'm hoping that means you're Everly Pauline Benedict."

"That's me." She cringed at hearing her middle name. "Most people call me Benny."

He stared at her. "Well...I'll be. You actually exist."

Benny didn't know what he meant by that. "Can I help you with something?"

"Actually, I'm here to help you." He placed a briefcase on the counter. "You, kid, just inherited a fortune."

TWO

BENNY

BOSTON, PRESENT DAY

Benny knew what an inheritance was—someone had left her money or a boat or a car (at least that's how it worked on *Lawyered Up*), but the question was who? Nobody Benny knew had money, but her mom seemed excited to hear the details, and Sal had said, "Kid, you're going to be rich!"

Benny wasn't so sure. What did this lawyer mean by "a fortune"? Did this have to do with whoever her father was? Benny had more questions than answers as she climbed the stairs to their sweltering apartment.

Sal had given her mom a couple of hours off so that she and Benny could meet with Peter Stapleton of Fineman, Larken, and Burr to discuss this inheritance business in private.

"I'm sorry for the mess." Benny's mom unlocked the door and ran to open the windows, while Benny turned on their lone fan. "We weren't expecting company, Mr. Stapleton."

Benny looked around the tiny apartment still full of boxes, some that hadn't even been unpacked at their last place in Vermont. (Benny had never been so grateful she'd remembered to do last night's dishes.)

"Please call me Peter, and don't apologize. I'm just happy I finally tracked you down." Peter grabbed an overturned box and sat down at the kitchen table. He removed his Yankees baseball cap. "You two move around a lot, and we're running out of time for you to collect the inheritance."

Her mom winked at her. "What can we say? Benny and I love new places. We don't like to be tied down."

Benny smiled wanly. After Grams had died, and her mom lost her job as an administrative assistant at a hospital in Toledo, her mom had declared it was time to start over. But when her mom lost her job in the next place, they moved again, and then again. Benny hated being the new girl at school all the time.

Peter removed a worn leather binder from his briefcase and pulled out a large stack of papers. "I've been looking for you two for two years. When we lost track of you in Ohio, it took almost a year to find you since you didn't register for a new license till you reached Vermont. And then you moved again. If you hadn't gotten a traffic ticket last week—"

Mom cut him off. "I did not roll through that stop sign. I swear."

"I'm glad you got the ticket, no offense," Peter said. "Before that I was ready to give up. The term of the inheritance trust ends in a little less than two weeks."

Two weeks? Benny picked up on that key phrase. "What do you mean the trust ends?"

Peter looked at her curiously. "This is going to sound odd, but to collect the inheritance, the benefactor created a game for you to play and the guidelines are very specific. You must start the game this June, and we've already lost a few days. The entire game must be completed by June twelfth."

"Game?" Benny sat up taller. Games were something she was good at.

"What did she inherit anyway?" Her mom frowned. "I hope I didn't lose an hour's pay to hear Benny is going to collect some sort of antique teapot."

He chuckled. "I can assure you, Ms. Benedict—Benny inherited more than a teapot. Your daughter just inherited an estate with a centuries-old inn and a vineyard worth millions."

Benny lost her balance, and her chair tipped straight over. Peter and her mom jumped, but Benny quickly recovered, scurrying to get up. "Did you...did you...just say *millions*? As in more than one million?" The words she was saying made no sense to her brain. Her mom understood. She started to scream.

Peter grinned. "Millions. Ever heard of Terry Estate Vineyards? No, of course not. You're a kid, but it's big and you're about to become the owner of that and Terry Inn Resort, the oldest inn in America. Forget the Hamptons. Terry Inn is the celebrity resort hot spot of the east end of Long Island."

"I've heard of both!" Her mom pulled the hair tie out of her ponytail—something she did when she was nervous. Her bangs fell in front of her eyes. "Are you saying Benny is now the owner? *We're* the owners?"

Benny felt her heart beating out of her chest. "This has to be a mistake," she said shakily, leaving all four feet of her chair on the floor. "Who would leave all this to me?"

"An ancestor by the name of Evelyn Terry." Peter put on reading glasses and consulted his papers. "She set up this trust for you specifically by name in 1850, the year our firm was established in New York."

Benny's stomach started to swirl. She knew that name from Grams. Her grandmother talked about her, calling Evelyn Terry "the first Evelyn." Grams loved talking about their ancestry and how someone named Evelyn was a legend in their family tree.

"Who is Evelyn Terry?" her mom asked, clearly never having had this conversation with Grams. "And how would she have left her fortune to Benny 175 years ago?"

"That's what we wanted to know!" Peter boomed. "Our firm has had a bet going forever about this. Evelyn's account is the oldest our firm has ever had, and the guidelines of her trust are very specific. The trust must be overseen by every firstborn in her family line from the date the trust was created till the time an Everly Benedict was to inherit it all in 2025." Peter took off his glasses. "Your mother, Evelyn Tate Benedict, never mentioned anything about this?"

The smile slid off Benny's mother's face. "What does my mother have to do with this?"

Peter put on his glasses again (black with blue sides, Benny noted). "She was the last Evelyn to serve on the Terry estate board, which oversees the trust."

"My mother?" Mom repeated thunderstruck. "No. My mother knew nothing about fancy vineyards or resorts, I can assure you."

Peter pushed a piece of paper across the table and pointed to Grams's name on the page. The paper was old and weathered, and it appeared to be a family tree listing women in their family line as far back as the early 1800s, starting with Evelyn Terry. "That's where you're wrong. I met your mother to discuss the trust several times when she came to New York City."

"That's impossible. My mother never even went to New York City!"

Yes, she did, Benny thought, biting the inside of her cheek. Grams always told Mom she was going away to a casino in Pennsylvania with girlfriends, but Benny knew the truth. *If you need me, I'll be at this hotel in New York*, she could recall her saying before giving Benny the number. *This is our secret, little guppy.* Which is what she called Benny on account of how much she loved the water.

"She was there, and she also knew the rules," Peter explained. "As long as the firstborn child born to someone in Evelyn Terry's direct line was named a variation of the name *Evelyn*, or *Evan* if it was a boy, they'd receive a stipend for sitting on the board while they were alive, helping the inn succeed and the vineyard, which was created in the last thirty years, continue to grow."

"Yes, yes, I know all about that stupid rule about being named *Evelyn*,'" Mom said, sounding agitated as she looked at Benny. "My mother said it was some sort of family superstition, like it was bad luck to not to have the name. That's why I'm a firstborn Evelyn—Evelyn Frances, but I always hated the name and insisted on being called Lynn. My mother and I fought about it for years until finally she said if I hated it so much, I could legally change it to Lynn, which I did when I was pregnant with Benny." She looked at Peter again, recognition starting to dawn on her. "And then she was the one who suggested I name my daughter *Everly*, as a compromise. I did, but always called her Benny, just to be difficult. Either way, I didn't know anything about any money or a board."

"Technically when you legally changed your name to Lynn, you forfeited your position with the Terry estate board," Peter said kindly. "Maybe that's why your mother never mentioned any of this. She didn't want to hurt your feelings."

"That sounds like my mother," Benny's mom said with a sigh.

Benny felt a prickling on the back of her neck and suddenly remembered something her grandmother used to tell her. *Someday, Benny, your ship is going to come in. You're going to have a bigger adventure than all of us, Guppy. Just you wait.* Benny didn't understand what she meant by that, but now she wondered: Did Grams mean this moment? Did Grams know the prediction? Was it really possible their ancestor Evelyn Terry had been waiting for Benny to be born, play the game, and collect the inheritance? *Her?* She was someone who blended into the background. She never stayed anywhere long enough to make friends. Her closest confidant had been her grandmother, and she'd been gone for years.

Benny's head was spinning. "Is there a reason the deadline is June twelfth?"

Peter made a face. "We haven't a clue."

A game with a very specific deadline. It made her even more curious. Benny started rattling off questions. "What about the game itself? Is there something specific I need to find? Or do? Are there clues?"

Peter started to laugh. "I'm glad you're excited to play, but this is the not-so-fun part of my job: telling you the rules. If you don't complete the game to the satisfaction of this agreement, you lose everything, and the Rudd family, who has the second-largest position on the estate board, and has invested a large sum of money in the winery and the inn over the years, can buy it out." He looked at her. "I've already heard from Vivian Rudd's lawyers. She's the matriarch of the family. There's no gray area in this, Benny. If you don't win the game, you'll get nothing."

That got Benny's blood pumping. She didn't know who this Vivian Rudd was, but she and her family weren't taking Benny's inheritance. "I know you don't know me, Peter, but I don't lose. I always play to win."

He smiled again. "That's what I wanted to hear."

"When can she start playing?" Mom asked.

"Immediately." Peter pulled out a map of New York's Long Island with several Xs on it. "To keep the inheritance, Evelyn Terry wants you to find an island off the coast of Long Island that doesn't exist on any maps. According to the trust, she's left you a series of riddles that should lead you to clues that will help you find the island."

Benny and her mom looked at each other in confusion.

"What do you mean, *find* it?" Mom said, saying what she was thinking. "If it's not on maps, what happened? Did the sea levels rise and flood it? Like with climate change or something?"

"Well...Evelyn left Benny a letter that is said to explain everything," Peter told them. "She was quite secretive, so they said, so it's remained sealed since the day she delivered it to the firm, but she claimed Benny would be able to locate the island if she found and followed the clues she left her and read her journal."

Benny and her mom stared closely at the yellowed map. On the east end of Long Island, where the land seemed to fork into two, there was a large bay with a red circle around a small section of the body of water. Scribbled in the center were two words: *Evelyn's Island.*

Benny pointed to the water. "And you're sure this is where this island is located?"

Peter shook his head. "We aren't. That's the thing—we've researched old maps and topographical studies, and there is nothing to indicate an island *ever* existed in this location. It has nothing to do with climate change. We've had surveyors check the surrounding area on multiple occasions, but we've never been able to locate an island anywhere."

That doesn't sound promising, Benny thought. *Be positive,* she reminded herself. *Evelyn wouldn't have created this game if it couldn't be won.*

"So we have to go to Long Island immediately in the hopes Benny can win this outlandish game?" Mom asked, now sounding skeptical. "I'm sorry, Peter." She glanced apologetically at Benny. "We don't have the money to go on a wild goose chase to find an island that doesn't exist. I have a job here. We have bills."

Rent, Benny remembered. They didn't have enough to pay their rent.

"Ah, well, that's the best part," Peter said, smiling again. "As long as Benny is playing the game, you may reside at the estate, you'll receive an allowance to live on, and all bills will be taken care of by the board. If she wins the game, she'll receive a considerable amount of money, plus ownership of the estate, the inn, and the vineyards. Honestly, you're set for life yourself if you invest wisely."

Benny and her mom were speechless. Benny wondered what her mom was thinking. She was afraid to sound too excited until she knew whether her mom was on board. If she had any chance of completing this game by the deadline, there was no time to lose. Her mom seemed lost in her thoughts. Benny watched as she played with a loose curl in her hair, pulling at it absentmindedly. Benny gave a tentative smile. "What do you think? It's kind of like a paid vacation." Her mom didn't say anything and that made Benny nervous. What if her mom said no? "And it's not like we have to stay on Long Island forever if we hate it." *If YOU hate it,* she thought. "The deadline for winning the game is in June."

Her mom sat up straighter and looked at her. "I know. You don't have a lot of time to pull this off. If we're going to give you your best shot we need to leave. Today." She jumped up and surprised Benny with a hug. "Let's go find your island!"

Benny felt like she might burst. "Let's!" Benny squeezed her mom back, her heart beating faster. Rent was no longer a problem. Not for this month. *I have to win. I have to. I can do this.*

"Splendid!" Peter slid over new papers where her signature was required. "Lynn, you'll still need to be on these papers as guardian because of Benny's age, but as of today, when you both sign these papers, Benny will take temporary ownership of Summerville—that's what they call the main house at Terry Inn Resort—the vineyards, *and* the island you have to find," Peter continued, ticking things off. "The family estate was built in the mid-1800s on the North Fork of Long Island, close to the water that supposedly overlooks the missing island, but it's been renovated extensively over the years." He slipped her a photograph of a large shaker-shingle Victorian house with several other cottages and buildings in the background. There was even a glimpse of a pool and the water beyond it.

"This is our house?" Benny's mom looked slightly ill. "In Greenport? New York?"

"That's the place," Peter said.

"Greenport." Mom picked up the photograph, and a strange look came over her face. "I've been there once before," she said softly. When she looked at Benny, her eyes were misty. "With your grandmother for a few days and... Never mind. It's a story for another time."

Benny wondered what her mother was referring to, but knowing her mom had been there, that her grandmother herself had left breadcrumbs, that her name was in these documents, sent a tingle down her spine. Grams knew about this. *Follow the clues,* she would say when they played games. *They'll give you the answers when you need them most, Guppy.*

Her heart thudded louder. It was wild but exciting. She was ready. "Do you have a pen?"

"Yes." Peter handed her what looked like a very expensive pen. It had heft to it when she picked it up to sign her name on the dotted line of each page. When she was finished, her mom cheered. Benny couldn't help but smile.

"Congratulations, Benny. Now it's time to give you this." Peter handed her a thick envelope that looked like it might disintegrate on the spot.

Benny took it from him and stared at her name written in a loopy script on the front of the envelope: *Everly Benedict*. She felt the hair on her neck stand up. "This is from Evelyn?"

"It is," Peter said, staring at the envelope. "We've had that letter in our possession for 175 years. I've always wondered what it said."

"Open it!" her mom insisted.

Benny took a deep breath, and Peter and her mother watched her carefully open the envelope. She got a whiff of the musty smell of old paper as she unfolded the letter. Several handwritten pages fell out. These were smaller papers that looked torn out from a book, and they looked even older than the letter. She read the top of the first page: *From Evelyn Terry's Private Journal*. The handwriting was a messier, more childish version of the writing on the envelope and the letter.

Benny was grateful that her grandmother had taught her how to read cursive.

She set the journal pages aside and picked up the letter. It was dated June 1850, and yet it was addressed to her. Goose bumps prickled her arms.

"What does it say?" her mom asked.

Benny read the first two lines twice to be sure she had them right.

> Dear Everly Benedict,
>
> I believe I am your great-great-great-great-great-grandmother, Evelyn Terry, and I've been waiting for you to break this curse for a very long time.

THREE

BENNY

PRESENT DAY

It had been mere hours since Benny agreed to play Evelyn's game, and now she and her mother were in their minivan packed with boxes. They were moving again. Her mom gave Sal notice immediately. There was no vacation time for a waitress on the job less than a month.

Truthfully, Benny didn't mind. She wasn't that attached to Boston—they'd been there less than a month, after her school year had ended in Vermont—but the thought of being homeless in a few weeks if she didn't find Evelyn's mysterious island made her feel queasy. The thrill of learning about the game, the inheritance, and Evelyn's letter had worn off slightly and now Benny was worried again.

Where would her mom move them next if this didn't work out?

"I'm excited. Are you excited? We're going to find this island together," Mom declared. "Be a team like you and your grandmother were when you played games." They were sitting in stalled traffic on the Long Island Expressway, two exits before it ended at exit 73. According to the GPS, they'd continue on for another thirty-five minutes to Greenport. "Won't that be fun?"

Benny had read and reread Evelyn's letter several times now, but she was no surer about how to find this island than she had been when Peter told her about the game. She'd read the journal pages too. The journal seemed to be from when Evelyn herself was twelve, and the few pages Benny had were about a day Evelyn and her friends had set out to visit their island—this sort of mystical-sounding place—when Evelyn met a strange man named Captain Jonas Kimble. Only Evelyn and her friend Aggy were able to see Captain Kimble and his vessel, which sounded like a pirate ship.

Was Evelyn for real with all this?

"Benny?" Mom prodded. "Isn't that a good idea? Us working together?"

"Yes," Benny said automatically, putting her feet up on the dash, the tips of her dirty white canvas sneakers staring back at her. Was it a good idea? She wasn't actually sure. Her mom tended to get distracted easily. She'd need to be laser focused to find this island. June twelfth was in a less than two weeks. That wasn't much time.

If she did find this island, their money woes would be over. But if she lost...

She wouldn't. She was no quitter.

"If you're going to help me, you should probably read Evelyn's letter," Benny added. "It gives the first riddle. And then there's her journal."

"Her journal..." Mom repeated, thinking. "What does she write about?"

"The pages I have are marked *Entry One*. She talks about the island. It almost sounds...fake," Benny admitted. "Sort of magical? This guy shows up and kind of shoos them away before they get to the island. I kind of get the feeling she thinks he's a pirate."

"A pirate," Mom repeated. "I didn't think there were still pirates around in the 1800s. At least not the kind you're thinking of."

"Neither did I," Benny agreed. These pages didn't give her much to go on. She wanted to read more of Evelyn's story, but according to Evelyn's letter, to do that, she'd have to solve the riddle to find the first clue.

"When we get to the house, you can borrow my phone and google *pirates of Long Island*," Mom suggested.

"That's a good idea." Benny couldn't wait to get her own phone—Peter had said they'd provide her with one when they got to Greenport.

Just then the traffic started to move again. "YES!" Mom shouted. "We'll be at Summerville House and the resort before you know it."

Let the game begin, Benny thought, and her fingers began to tingle. What exactly was she getting herself into? *A new house*, she told herself again. *A place with air-conditioning. Possibly a new car.* She'd believe anything Evelyn wrote if it meant making these things happen.

A few minutes later, they were off the highway, driving past an outlet mall and every box store she could imagine. Soon the stores gave way to farmland and open fields where grape vines grew on trellises in long rows. Horses and cows grazed in the distance, and signs for various vineyards began appearing.

"Why don't you read me the letter aloud?" Mom suggested. "And don't forget the riddle."

Benny pulled the letter and the journal pages out of her backpack again. The backpack was loaded with her most prized possessions. She didn't have much. There was a small wooden bird her father supposedly carved for her mother when they dated, and her travel games, like Scrabble and Tenzi. A book of crossword puzzles she'd gotten at the thrift store. A worn paperback copy of *Ready Player One*, which was her favorite book, even though it was superlong. Patiently, Benny read aloud:

Dear Everly Benedict,

I believe I am your great-great-great-great-great-grandmother, Evelyn Terry, and I've been waiting for you to break this curse for a very long time.

This letter will be difficult to comprehend, but I've taken careful measures to ensure my inheritance is left to you. To collect it, however, you'll need to play my game and complete it by June 12, 2025. The objective? Find something very important to me—an island that has been lost to the world. This task may seem impossible, but I know you can do it.

I've written an entire journal explaining what happened in the days leading up to the island's disappearance. For reasons I can't disclose in this letter, I have divided the journal up. Each time you decode another riddle in my game, you'll receive more pages from my journal. Everything fantastical I've written in this journal actually happened. And everything that happened is my fault. But all is not lost. Knowing you will come along someday has given me hope.

I know now that you can break the curse.

Find the island.

Save them.

All of them.

I'm counting on you.

With deep love and

admiration,

Evelyn Terry

Here is your first riddle:

Treasure, the object of this game,
Waits on an island with no name.
Find one or two of my favorite tomes
Sitting somewhere in my home.
Take care to read behind the lines
For that first clue, so bound to find.

"Wow," Mom said, her eyes on the road. "When Peter said Evelyn wanted you to find an island, he really meant it. This isn't going to be easy."

"No," Benny admitted. "But she wants me to win, right? So I'm sure each clue she left me will lead me closer to finding it." *I hope.*

"Yes, but what does she mean by a curse? Or *save them?*" Mom asked. "Save who?"

"I don't know," Benny said, looking at Evelyn's handwriting again. "The letter is confusing. She seems afraid to say too much. And the first pages of her journal don't talk about anyone needing rescuing." Benny assumed there had to be more Evelyn wasn't telling her yet. She had to assume the first clue would offer more insight and journal pages. She just had to find what Evelyn had hidden. "I'm just going to focus on the first riddle. Clearly, she wants me to find one or two of her favorite books, right?"

She looked out the car window at a beautiful robin's-egg blue wooden sign hanging on a large shingle: *Terry Inn Resort, two miles ahead. Terry Estate Vineyards, straight ahead.* Benny looked at the letter again and bit her lower lip. She still felt like she was missing something. What did Evelyn mean by *break the curse?* She wrestled with the riddle for a few minutes till she heard the GPS say, *"Your destination is on the right."*

Benny sat up straight when she saw it. "Hold up! That's our house?"

Mom screamed, "Yes!" She took one hand off the wheel and shook Benny's shoulder. "That's our house!"

The minivan reached the end of the long driveway, and Mom cut the engine. To their right was a path to the Terry Inn Resort, and to their left was the house. Benny recognized Summerville from Peter's photo, but in person, it was even more stunning. It had gabled roofs, bay windows, and two brick chimneys nestled on either side of a rooftop patio. Several porches and balconies overlooked the waterfront behind the house, and in the distance, they saw two pools—one at the inn and one at the main house.

Benny and her mom looked at each other and jumped out of the car. Mom's eyes filled with tears. "Benny... This is our *house*," she repeated.

They'd never had a house of their own before. They'd rented an apartment on the first floor of a house with Grams, and when she'd passed away, they'd rented apartment after apartment in large buildings, never having a place to truly call home. Benny bit her lower lip to keep from crying herself. *This is our house...for now. If I don't find the island, Evelyn takes it all away.*

"Welcome!" The voice was clipped and Benny detected with a hint of a British accent.

Benny and her mom turned to the front door, where an older gentleman was waiting for them. Benny quickly sized him up: in his sixties, salt-and-pepper hair, cared about appearances (he was wearing khaki pants and a sweater vest in June). Maybe he also liked birds, since a small black bird was embroidered on his vest pocket.

"Am I to assume you are the new lady of the house?" he asked, looking directly at Benny.

Benny looked at her mother, who was wiping her eyes. "We both are."

The man smiled. "Noted. Lynn and Everly 'Benny' Benedict, I presume?"

"That's us," Benny said. "And you are?"

The man's blue eyes looked almost as gray as the clouds that speckled the sky (it looked like it might rain). "Wallace Ingram, but you can call me Wally. I am the caretaker of the main house. Summerville has been awaiting your arrival for a long time."

GREENPORT HERALD

June 7, 1825

COUGH PLAGUES GREENPORT

BY ABIGAIL JONES

Several businesses and the Greenport schoolhouse are closed indefinitely due to the outbreak of the Cough. Several families in Greenport have fallen ill in the last few days. Many more are believed to be in quarantine. A full account of the dead is not yet known, but it is believed that several have already died from illness.

Greenport does not want to see a repeat of the Yellow Fever epidemic that plagued New York in the late 1700s and 1803, and felled thousands of people. Measures must be taken to prevent further disease. Elias Rudd has closed the port and is having vessels checked before entry for ill passengers and deliveries. Villagers are urged to remain at home if they can.

FOUR

BENNY

PRESENT DAY

As they explored the house, Benny's mom was like a kid in a candy store, running from room to room, shouting about the home's magazine-ready décor.

"Two fireplaces? *Three*? Oh, Benny, wait till you see this room! Look at this kitchen! And the hot tub!"

Benny was more tentative, slipping off her sneakers and placing them by the front door, afraid to get dirt on all those white surfaces. From the two-story entrance hall, she could see a wall of French doors leading out to a backyard. She'd never been in a house that had a name before—*Summerville*. Benny tried not to let herself feel as excited as Mom was.

This wasn't their house yet.

It could be, but for now, it was a vacation, and they never got to take vacations. Benny took in the rustic wood beams, wide central staircase, the old paintings and portraits lining the walls, and tried to imagine how it all fit into Evelyn's game. Where were Evelyn's favorite books? They could be anywhere in a house this large. She needed to focus, not fall in love with a house that might not be hers to keep.

"What do you think? It's a stunning home, isn't it?"

The voice speaking was different from Wally's, and Benny turned to see who it was. The man standing in the kitchen was balding, with a deep voice, a nice smile, and blue eyes. He wore a suit that seemed even nicer than the one Peter the lawyer wore. As the man approached, Benny got a whiff of pine, which always reminded her of the holidays.

Her mom, who had been wandering the other rooms, came in just then. "Benny, Wally says the resort pool also has a jacuzzi, and I could swear I just saw Taylor Swift in—" She stopped when she saw the man. "Oh, hello." She moved a loose strand of brown hair behind her right ear and smiled.

Oh no, Benny thought. *I know that look.*

"You must be Evelyn," said Harris and offered her mom his hand.

"It's Lynn now," her mom said with a bashful laugh, and Benny tried not to grimace.

"Lynn suits you," he said. "I'm Harris Gale." He turned to Benny. "And you must be the famous Everly." He offered his hand to give her a warm handshake. "We have been waiting to meet you for what feels like forever."

"You can call me Benny," she said.

"Harris is a board member for the Terry Estate," Wally told them. "He wanted to be here to answer any questions you might have about the vineyards or the inn. He is actually an investor in the vineyard and owns several businesses in Greenport."

"Oh!" Mom's voice lifted. "Several businesses?"

"Wally is making me sound like a bigger deal than I am," Harris said. "I'm no Vivian Rudd. That woman owns everything in this town." A flicker crossed his face that Benny couldn't decipher. "Anyway, I'm here because we want you both to feel right at home."

"We appreciate that," her mom said, her voice sort of velvety. "I can't imagine a more beautiful place."

Harris nodded. "Well, we have Evelyn to thank for that. She established the Terry Inn in 1835, and it soon thrived. Several presidents have stayed here over the years. And the vineyard started with a grapevine her father planted."

Evelyn mentioned the grapevine in her journal, Benny

realized. *And if that is real, why can't the island be too?* The vines had grown into something that was still here. It gave her hope.

"Eventually Evelyn built Summerville," Harris continued. "Then her grandchildren took over the inn and expanded it. But it all started with Evelyn's smart business skills. It's amazing to think about everything she accomplished, and how she put plans in motion that we are carrying out today," he said, looking at Benny.

"So the board knows about the game Evelyn left me?" Benny asked. He nodded.

"What are your thoughts on this missing island business?"

"Well..." Harris paused, then cleared his throat. "It does sound difficult. Having you follow clues to find an island that no one has ever even heard of? And if you don't, you lose the inheritance?" He shook his head. "That sort of plan makes a businessman like me nervous."

Benny couldn't say he was wrong about that. Her eye caught a small painting on the wall behind Harris's head. It looked similar to a bird statue on one of the tables in the foyer. Actually, there were several bird items in the house in addition to the one on Wally's shirt. What was that about?

"We all want you to win, Benny," Harris said softly. "So

that what we built here doesn't fall into the hands of Vivian Rudd's' family. That's the family that will take over the inn and vineyard should you fail."

The Rudds. Benny remembered the name from Peter and the paperwork she'd signed.

Harris clasped his hands together. "So let's make sure that doesn't happen."

"It won't," Benny and her mom said at the same time. They smiled at each other. For once, Benny felt they were in sync.

"Good! Well, I'm sure you'd like to settle in. May I suggest the master bedroom with the covered balcony? That is everyone's favorite," Harris told Mom. As he unclasped his hands, Benny noticed he wasn't wearing a wedding ring. "Summerville has been a vacation house for some of our more exclusive guests." He leaned in. "You wouldn't believe who has stayed here. Wally could tell you stories."

Her mom's eyes lit up, and she turned to Wally. "Really? Like who?"

"I shouldn't say," Wally said politely.

"*I* could be persuaded though," Harris said, winking at Mom and making her laugh. "In fact, if you have time, I could give you a tour of the vineyard right now."

Benny tried to catch her mom's eye, hoping she'd get the message: *We have a deadline here.*

But her mom smiled back at Harris. "That would be wonderful!" Then she turned to Benny. "Do you want to come along?"

Benny shook her head. "No, thanks, but you should go if you want." She didn't want to spoil her mom's mood, even though she secretly wished she'd stay and help with the riddle. "Mr. Gale and I won't be long," she called as she headed to the door with Harris right behind her.

The door shut, and then it was just Benny and Wally and the whir of the air-conditioning.

She was on her own. Again.

"Well," said Wally. "Let's find you a room, shall we?"

"Any room is fine. I don't care where I sleep," Benny told him. She wasn't going to be spending too much time in her room if she had clues to crack. Benny grabbed her camera, ready to take pictures of anything of interest with a fresh roll of film.

"I think I know the perfect one," he said, his eyes twinkling as he headed for the stairs.

"Can I ask you something?" she asked Wally, following him. "Any idea why the game deadline is June twelfth of this year?"

"I am sure there must be a reason." His hazy blue eyes

were warm, the weathered lines on his face reminding her he'd lived to see many people come and go in this house over the years. He paused on the stair landing to stare out a window at the bay. "Whether anything is really out there, I don't know, but I've been in this house long enough to know if there's really an island, Evelyn left you a way to find it. There are those on the board who think this is a fool's errand—leaving you an inheritance with such strict stipulations. But I choose to believe in the original lady of this house. She was convinced the island existed. And sometimes, when you believe hard enough, it becomes your reality." Wally pushed open the door at the end of the upstairs hallway. "And if you are going to think like Evelyn, maybe you should stay in her original room."

Benny inhaled sharply. Evelyn's room was the size of their entire apartment in Boston, with its own bathroom and a large sitting area with a small bookcase tucked into an alcove. She snapped a picture and made a memory with her mind. "It's beautiful," Benny said, taking in the comfy-looking bed with its numerous pillows, the TV on the wall, and the big window perfect for looking out at the water. There was even a small balcony beyond a set of French doors. As Benny looked around, her stomach started to churn like the small white-capped waves on the shore. *Don't get attached.*

"This window is perfectly situated for a view of the

lighthouse," Wally pointed out. Benny could see the silhouette of an offshore lighthouse in the distance. "Evelyn commissioned that lighthouse with President Andrew Jackson's blessing, in fact," Wally said.

"You're kidding. That's cool," Benny said.

"It is cool," Wally noted. "It's been standing since 1850. But there's not much use for a lighthouse in between Long Island's two forks anymore, so it went out of commission years ago. It's a museum now, run by the Greenport Historical Society. If you go, ask for Thea Dabney."

"Thea Dabney." Benny made a mental note to remember the name. Maybe she knew something about Evelyn that could be useful.

"Come see the balcony." Wally opened the French doors. "Once you see this view, you won't be able to refuse this room."

Benny stepped outside with him. The balcony wasn't large enough for more than a single chair, but the view was spectacular.

"Lots of coastal homes from this time period had balconies that faced the sea, in order to watch for ships," he explained. "I suspect with Evelyn's history, she used this balcony to search for something else."

The island, Benny thought, watching clouds roll in fast. It looked like it might rain.

"You can look over the entire estate from here," Wally added. "All five hundred acres, most of which Evelyn kept for farmland while she was alive." He pointed out to the grounds on the left. "Out that way is the town. The Rudds owned most of it when Evelyn was young, but later she bought quite a bit of property there, including the spot where Hooked Restaurant now stands." He sighed. "Later, the Rudds bought that space back and built Hooked. Evelyn would have hated that, but it was after she passed. She wasn't a fan of the Rudds, and the feeling was mutual."

The Rudds again. Benny made a note to learn more about them too.

"So? Shall we call this your room?" he asked. "This view alone makes it worth it."

It *was* nice, but... "Are you sure? It's more than I need, and I don't want to get too attached in case..." Benny trailed off. *What if I'm only here for two weeks?* was her first thought. Her second was Grams's voice in her head scolding her, *Guppy, you can do this! You can do anything!*

"You don't find the island and can't stay?" Wally guessed. "I wouldn't worry. You're going to find it. Let's have hope, shall we?"

"You're right," Benny agreed. "Okay. I'll take it." She took a picture of the view. "And now that my room is settled, maybe you can help me with something else."

"Anything," Wally told her.

"Where can I find books that might have belonged to Evelyn?" she asked hopefully.

Wally smiled. "Did I mention the house has a private library?"

FIVE

BENNY

PRESENT DAY

Benny bounded back down the stairs with Wally at her heels. "You should have told me about the library first! Which way is it?" *Imagine I solve this whole game in one afternoon!* she thought.

"Down the hall to the left. And you didn't ask about a library till just now." Wally chuckled.

Benny took the stairs two at a time, her heart racing as she turned and headed down the hall. "I know! Sorry!" She was getting excited. "Is it a big library? Because I need to find two of Evelyn's favorite books. You wouldn't happen to know what they were, would you?"

"I'm afraid not," Wally told her. "But if that book is

anywhere, it's probably here. Evelyn was a voracious reader, and the library has thousands of books in its collection."

Benny stopped short. "*Thousands?*" That was going to be a lot of books to sort through.

"Oh yes," Wally told her. "It is a collection of the Terry family's books and new ones for guests. We also have several bound volumes of the town's first newspaper, the *Greenport Herald*. There are several articles that mention Evelyn over the years, if you want to find out more about her." He reached the door at the end of the hall. "Here we are."

Every wall of the library was covered in mahogany bookcases that reached to the ceiling, their shelves filled with books of various shapes and sizes, many of them leather bound. Each wall had an iron library ladder on a rolling track to let someone retrieve books from higher shelves. The room was slightly musty, the smell of leather and old books permeating the air.

"This room is original to the house," Wally told her. "When Evelyn left the house to her children, her will stipulated that the bookcases stay in place, with no new walls or expansions to the room. I'm glad for that—she always wanted to keep this room as a library."

Benny touched some of the spines—a mix of old and new before her—and looked around for clues. The room had two large wingback chairs and a bench below the one window. A single wooden clock with a strangely numbered face sat on the mantel. It had a picture of a small village on a beach below the clockface. The clock ticked quietly.

"I've never seen a clock like this before," Benny said, peering at it closely.

"It's a tide clock. Been in that spot as long as I've been working here."

Interesting. Benny moved on, observing the one wall that was without shelves. Instead, it featured a large bay window situated above a built-in bench overlooking a garden, the sky above it darkening with the approaching storm. On either side of the window were paintings and portraits.

"That one right there is a portrait of Evelyn." Wally pointed to one of a young girl. "She painted this one in her thirties, but it's a self-portrait of herself at your age. I think I can see a resemblance."

In the painting, Evelyn stood knee-deep in stormy water. Her long brown hair was wild, a blue dress billowing around her, the hem of which appeared wet from the sea spray. The water looked rough; the sky was dark, a crackling of lightning across the sky. Her eyes seemed to be staring directly at Benny from the canvas in a way that was almost unnerving. Benny wasn't sure if she could see the resemblance, but there was something in the girl's eyes—fire, determination, a certain playfulness, all wrapped into one that Benny could appreciate. She knew each of these traits well.

Hi there, Evelyn, Benny said to the girl in the painting. *I'm here to play your game. Where is your first clue hiding?*

"She also did a painting of an island," Wally said, interrupting her thoughts.

Benny did a double take. "Where?"

Wally tapped a smaller painting on the wall.

Benny frowned. The island didn't look like one here in the Northeast. This one had white sand, a colorful bird in one of the trees, and turquoise water. The sun was shining brightly, casting a ray on a cave located on the beach. And was that a fort? Evelyn's journal didn't mention a fort. She made it sound like she was the first person to find the island. Hmm. Benny searched the painting for clues. Evelyn had painted five people on the beach, all in silhouette. The painting reminded her of a Monet—all soft lines, no edges, like a picture out of focus or a memory. She looked at Wally. "May I lift it off the wall?"

"Be my guest."

Benny held her breath as she lifted the frame and examined the back and the wall behind it. She'd been hoping for a secret safe or a message, but there was nothing there. She glanced at the self-portrait again. *Evelyn, help me win.* "Who are the other pictures and paintings of?" she asked, putting the painting back on the hook.

Wally looked up at the wall. "That is your family tree."

Family. With Grams gone, Benny didn't have much of that. It was her and Mom. Benny stared at the black-and-white photographs of women with children riding horses, at the beach standing next to large black dogs, standing on the balcony of a lighthouse in awe. Some of the women in the photos were children, others were young adults or seniors, but Benny noticed they all had that same fire in their eyes.

"Every generation that has come before you is on that wall," Wally added, smiling up at the wall. "Seven, if my math is right."

"Seven?" Benny was about to try to do the math herself when she saw a picture that looked very familiar. "Grams," she whispered, goose bumps trailing her arms as her fingers traced the black-and-white image of a small girl in a one-piece bathing suit sitting on a dock, her arms around a shaggy brown dog. Grams couldn't be older than eight in this picture, but she remembered Grams showing her a similar picture once. *I was always fiery,* she'd said. *Like you. I liked adventure.*

Grams knew, Benny thought. She knew this adventure was in her future, and she'd kept the secret safe her whole life. If there was ever a question of whether Benny belonged here, this photograph answered it.

A loud rumble of thunder seemed to make the whole house shake. Seconds later, she could hear the rain, as if it were moving over the house, pelting the roof. She hoped Mom and Harris weren't getting soaked right now.

"Guess we'll have to wait to show you the gardens," Wally said. "I think you'll like them. There's a sunken garden with a wooden gate that leads from Summerville to the inn. There's even a purple wisteria on the grounds that Evelyn herself supposedly planted."

Benny felt something stir inside of her. She wasn't sure if it was the thrill of cracking the case, the game afoot, or this house. This place. Why did she feel like she belonged here? She tried to push the thought aside. *Don't get attached* she reminded herself, even as she looked to Wally, someone she had a feeling she could trust. And trust was something she didn't do easily.

Lightning lit up the great room, and Wally moved to turn on some of the lamps. The rain was coming down hard. "Perfect weather for exploring a big new house, if you ask me." He pulled a bound copy of *Greenport Herald* 1825–1830 off one of the shelves. "Also great weather for reading."

Benny hugged the book to her chest. It smelled like leather and was heavier than any textbook she'd read in school. She looked around again. The answers to the riddle were here. Right in front of her. She just had to find them.

ENTRY 2

From Evelyn Terry's Private Journal,
Dated June 4, 1825

> Aggy and I were the only ones who saw the man and the pirate ship that night! Our friends were standing right there, but they saw nothing and thought we were acting strangely...

"Are you two alright?" Thomas asked, spying Aggy and me still standing at the water's edge.

"We're fine," I said, startled. "We'll see you tomorrow at school."

"See you tomorrow," Gil called to us. "Get home before the storm!"

Gil, Thomas, and Laurel headed in one direction, and Aggy and I went in the other. We were both quiet for a bit, the sound of the trees whipping like a whistle to keep us company.

Aggy finally spoke. "I know you saw the ship. Just as I did."

I felt myself inhale sharply. If Aggy saw it too, then I wasn't seeing things. Aggy has the gift of sight, according to her mama. That means she can "see" things that will happen before they do. "Don't walk the main road today, Sparrow," she'll say, and then someone will die when their wagon overturns on that very road. "Don't let your father plow tomorrow," she told me last week. Mr. Jones three farms away sliced off two of his fingers in a plow accident the next day. No one else knows about her gift but her mom and her aunt, who lives with them since Aggy's father died a few years back. That's why they moved to Greenport. Aggy's mom and aunt are healers, but neither have the gift of sight, according to Aggy.

My heart was thumping now. "Does that mean...? Do you think...? If the others didn't see the man or the ship, and I did, does that mean I have the gift of sight too?"

Aggy pulled at the white knotted string tied on her pale wrist. I wore one just like it. We'd made them one afternoon together. "No. I think you saw him because you *chose* to, just like you chose to find the island."

"What does that mean?" I asked, confused. "Was he a spirit?"

"No," Aggy said decidedly. "He was real. He was just...a man out of time."

"I don't understand what you're saying," I told her, my tone impatient. While I love my friend, she sometimes speaks in riddles and acts much older than me, even though we're roughly the same age. (She's thirteen, I'm twelve—so we get along like fireflies.) It helps she's easy to talk to, we both like to swim, and both like to write. But sometimes her gift means she speaks about things I do not understand.

"Your father is coming," Aggy said quietly, her blue dress whipping around her. "I will tell you more about this another time. Just promise me, Sparrow. You won't talk to anyone about meeting that man tonight."

I stopped short, my bare feet sinking into the mud beneath my toes. "Why can't I tell anyone about him?"

Aggy was quiet for a moment. "Because people won't understand. Not yet." She struggled to find the right words, it seemed. "Our friends will in time, but if you try to tell them now, it will only frighten them about what comes next."

I stepped closer to her. "What comes next?" My friend

looked everywhere but at me. "Does this have anything to do with the Blood Orange Moon?"

I saw something sorrowful in her eyes, but just then I heard someone whistling. It wasn't Papa. I stiffened. Axel Rudd was walking down the path toward us.

With his dark hair and even darker eyes, there was something about Axel that always bothered me. Unlike the rest of us, Axel didn't wear hand-me-downs from his siblings or have a mother who sewed his clothes. His came from England (as he repeatedly told us), and he and his brothers had several shirts that they wore each week, whereas I had only the two dresses I wore all year. He was the same age as Gilbert, yet he was markedly different, a smug fellow who thought he was so sharp because his father owned most of Greenport and the factory on the wharf.

"Good evening, Axel," I said politely.

"Evelyn," he said smoothly.

He is the only one of our friends who doesn't call me by my nickname. He says it is stupid. Since this is my story to tell, I can say I sometimes think Axel is stupid too.

"I came calling on you, Evelyn, and your father said you were out in the fields, yet I went looking and didn't find you." His eyes glinted sharply. "Instead, I find you here with Aggy. Where are you both coming from?"

"We were taking an evening walk," I told him.

He cocked his head. "In the rain?" We didn't answer him. He narrowed his eyes. "Were you on the island?" He could never find his way there on his own.

"No," we said at the same time, which only made us look guilty.

Axel folded his arms across his chest. "What are you two up to?"

For someone who goaded us about how he would some-day own this town, he sure hated to be left out of things.

"Nothing," we said again in unison, which made things worse.

"Evelyn! Evelyn, where are you?"

"Papa," I whispered. Aggy was right. My father was look-ing for me. "I should go."

"So should I," Aggy said, not wanting to be left alone with Axel. "Sparrow, we'll talk in the morning? On the way to school?" Her expression was pointed. *Say nothing about tonight to your parents.*

"I will wait for you at your garden gate," I told her. "The one by the rosemary." I looked at Axel again. "Good night."

"Good night," he said stiffly, watching us both go.

I ran ahead, mad at myself for my appearance and for having to explain my lack of shoes. "I'm here, Papa!" I said, my empty bucket and the lantern I carried bouncing as I ran.

"Evelyn!" Papa said, hugging me. "Your mother and I were getting so worried when you didn't come back. And then Axel Rudd came calling on you."

"I'm sorry, Papa. I didn't mean to make you worry. And I wouldn't call it a calling," I said stiffly. Axel and I are not mutually smitten with one another. I shuddered at the thought. "I went to see Aggy." That part was the truth.

Papa chuckled. "We won't tell your mother that part. You know she worries about you catching your death in the cold."

Mama worries about us getting ill a lot. Three members of the Davies family died a few weeks ago from pertussis, and the Miller girl is said to have it at the farm one road over from us now. Mama is terrified the Cough will strike our home next. Once someone has the Cough, it is hard to keep away. "I feel fine, Papa," I promised.

"Even so, you're going to have a hard time explaining your lack of shoes and soiled dress from checking on my grapes."

My cheeks burned. "I will check on them first thing."

He hugged me to his side. "That is fine, my darling girl." Mama says he is too soft with me. "Everything alright with Aggy?"

"Yes, Papa."

I could feel the temperature dropping, and there was a

sudden shift in the wind. We both looked up at the dark clouds overtaking the night sky.

Papa frowned. "This weather troubles me."

His fears were my chance at asking him something. "Papa, do you think a Blood Orange Moon is causing the change in weather?"

Papa studied me as we started the walk down the road to our farmhouse. "Where did you hear about that? Mama said not to tell you about it. She didn't want you to get scared."

"I don't get scared," I said, which is true.

When the storm started earlier tonight, it was a wicked one. It blew in out of nowhere after supper; the wind so fierce it took the shutters off our house, snapped trees like twigs. The thunder was loud enough to rattle windows and make lightning fork through the sky like a river splitting into multiple paths. "You can tell me the truth."

"I believe it is the Blood Orange Moon," Papa admitted. "The *Farmers' Annual* predicted it coming. It's when a lunar eclipse, a second full moon in one calendar month, and an orange moon—when the sun and moon appear in the sky at the same time—all occur on the same night. We haven't seen a moon occurrence like it in two hundred years."

I always like when Papa pulls out his worn copy of the *Farmers' Annual*, something he reads even more than the Bible, and explains different passages. "Is a Blood Orange Moon a bad thing?"

"Well, the *Annual* says it can usher in strange occurrences," Papa said, watching the wind blow through the trees. "It can destroy crops, change tides, cause rough seas and storms, make animals go mad. Some of the farmers I've spoken to have called this type of moon a curse. It certainly is a bad omen."

I suddenly felt cold. And now this strange man had appeared right around the same time I found the island, and he spoke of the very same celestial occurrence. "Are you worried?"

"Some," Papa said and wrapped an arm around me. "Best thing we can hope for is that the calamities of the Blood Orange Moon pass Greenport by." He hugged me tighter. "Now tell me truly: Where did you and Aggy run off to tonight?"

I couldn't lie to my papa. I never have been able to. "Our island. The one near the beach you can get to at the fork in the road between Aggy's house and our farmhouse? By the tulip tree? A few paces away from the road that leads into town. It's hard to find. Covered by brush by the beach, but I found it a few weeks ago, and whenever we arrive, there is a sandbar that lets us walk across to it. We've been going there when we can to explore."

JEN CALONITA

Papa stared at me a moment, then started to chuckle. "Oh, darling girl, what an imagination you have. The only islands off Greenport are Gardiner's and Shelter Island. And I highly doubt you would have made it to either of them by foot. There is no sandbar off Greenport."

Papa was wrong. There *is* an island. I've been there. Seen it with my own eyes, but the way my father was looking at me, I was afraid to say more. I was even more nervous to ask him my next question. "Papa, have you ever heard of a man named Captain Jonas Kimble?"

"Ah, Miss Talbert is teaching you local history in school, is she?" Papa asked.

My heart seized. "You know who he is?"

"Of course. One of the most famous pirates to sail these waters in the 1600s." Papa smiled. "Legend has it, he buried some of his treasure right here in Greenport. It's never been found though. Would be nice to have all that gold, wouldn't it?"

My heart was beating faster now, my hands growing clammy. "Did you say he lived in the 1600s? Two hundred years ago?"

"Yes, dear girl, why?" Papa wanted to know.

I felt dizzy at the thought. The wind rushed by us then, practically pushing us down the path, and I felt like I heard

72

voices again. It was the island. I was sure of it, and it was singing my name.

Evelyn. Evelyn Terry. Welcome home.

"No reason," I whispered. "No reason at all."

SIX

BENNY

It rained for the next three days straight. Three days of sitting in the library, removing random books from shelves, checking publication dates to see if Evelyn could have read them, or whether she left any notes tucked into their pages. Benny got excited when she found books from Evelyn's time period: *Pride and Prejudice, Great Expectations,* and *Jane Eyre.* But none of these books had any markings in them or clues inside. These must not have been Evelyn's favorites. There were other books too: bound volumes of the *Greenport Herald,* which Wally gave her, nautical tide charts, and books on growing grapes. Benny wondered if she would have to go through every single book in the library. How long would that take? Time was one thing she didn't have a lot of.

As anxious as she was, she'd never been so pampered before. She slept in a four-poster bed with the softest sheets, her laundry was magically taken care of, and piping-hot chocolate chip pancakes awaited her in the kitchen in the morning. Mom had no more double shifts or dark shadows under her eyes. Instead, each morning she'd grab an umbrella and venture out into Greenport with Harris as her tour guide ("If you need me, I'll be back right away," she'd say), and Benny would just let her go. She liked seeing her mom happy. Even if her own stress level was growing.

She tried not to enjoy the fact there was a living room, a great room, *and* a den, all of which had TVs, one bigger than the next, which meant she and Mom didn't have to argue over what they were watching. They could each stream their own show. Separately if they wanted! When Mom was there, they stretched out their legs and laid on couches that were so thick and cozy, sometimes Benny fell asleep on them, the sound of rain softly hitting the windows and doors. Outside, the June air was getting stickier and steamier, but inside the house, the air was so cool Benny sometimes reached for a blanket, which was ironic considering in Boston, she would have given her right arm to be cold. Was it possible to be spoiled by central air in just a few days?

She explored the house looking for other books, examined

knickknacks that looked ancient, and took pictures off walls to see if there was anything taped to the back. Benny tried all the usual mystery-movie sorts of clues, but she kept coming up empty.

What if I don't solve this riddle? she worried. *What if all this goes away?*

You have less than two weeks, she thought as she tried to retrieve a copy of *The Great Gatsby* from a high shelf in the den. The step stool she was standing on wasn't very steady at all.

Behind her, Wally cleared his throat. "Benny, I hate to tell you this, but that stool isn't meant for reaching high places."

Mom came in the room and gasped. "Benny, get down from there."

"I'm fine!" *I almost have it,* she thought. Her fingers caught the small black bird bookend instead and it started to teeter before it fell. Her mom caught the bookend before it hit the floor.

"Get down! You're going to break your neck," Mom scolded.

"Sorry! I needed that book," Benny told them, grabbing the book and climbing down. She wiped her dusty hands off on her shorts and cracked open *The Great Gatsby* then gave a weary sigh. "This isn't the book I'm looking for. It was published in 1925."

"It's a good book though, if you haven't read it," Wally said kindly.

"So many items with black birds in this house," her mom noted, looking at the bookend as she handed it to Wally. "Is there a reason?"

Benny froze. Her mom might be on to something. "Is it because Evelyn's nickname is Sparrow?"

"Possibly," Wally said. "I am told Evelyn was a big fan of the bird." He pointed to the insignia on his vest. "The sparrow is even part of our logo."

"I don't suppose there are any famous books about sparrows, are there?" Benny pulled her new phone out of her pocket to check. No. The only sparrow she could find was a fictional character, Captain Jack Sparrow.

"You need to get out of this house," Mom said. "You've been reading books for days!"

"Wally, you hear this? My mom is complaining I'm reading," Benny teased.

"You know what I mean," Mom said. "You need air. You've got plenty of time to figure out the riddle, honey. You need to clear your head. Go swimming! It's overcast, but it's not raining today. Or take a bike and go into town. It's darling—lots of little shops. I think there's a Mexican place, a hot sauce store, *and* a cookie shop that specializes in blue duck cookies.

All your favorite things. Well, not the blue ducks, but... Tell her, Wally."

"Your mother is right," Wally agreed. "See the town. Meet people your own age instead of hanging out with us old folk."

Mom mock gaped. "Speak for yourself, Wally." They both laughed.

"Do you want to come with me?" *We're running out of time,* Benny wanted to say.

Her mom's smile faltered. "Harris was going to take me on a drive to Orient Point to see a new restaurant his company just opened; I'll tell him no."

You look so happy, Benny thought. *And this is the first normal guy you've dated in years.* "No, you go. I'll bike to town for an hour. *Tops.*" Benny dared her mom to try to argue that point. "You're both probably right; I should clear my head."

Her mom raised one eyebrow. "One more round before we both go?"

"Of course." Benny didn't have to ask what her mother meant. She followed her into the kitchen where there was a Scrabble board with a game already in play. It was her mom's turn. Benny watched as she placed a four-letter word on the board.

Benny went next. *T-O-M-E* for six points. Books were the

only thing on her mind at the moment. Evelyn's favorite books. Where were they? *What* were they?

"You're winning as usual." Mom went to the cabinet with the big plastic cups, then moved to the fridge to use the ice maker. Benny felt her stomach tighten. Her mom knew her way around this kitchen already. "And you're going to crack this riddle any day now." She leaned on the counter and looked at her. "But you need to give yourself a break sometimes or you won't be able to think clearly."

"I know! I just feel like I've gotten nowhere and the clock is ticking." Benny felt her shoulders tense. She glanced outside. It wasn't raining, but it looked like it was going to storm again.

"Put yourself in Evelyn's shoes," her mom suggested. "Where would she go if she wanted to clear her head?

"The island?" Benny guessed. "But since I can't do that, maybe I'll go to the historical society." The museum had to have information on Evelyn. She looked at Wally. "Who did you say I should ask for there?"

Mom groaned. "More history? Who is this child who thinks of nothing but work?"

"Thea Dabney," Wally told her. "Bikes are in the garage."

"A *three*-car garage," Mom said giddily as Benny headed for a side door. "Don't forget your new cell phone. So I know where you are."

Benny grabbed the phone off the counter—the only three numbers she had in the thing were mom's, her lawyer's, and Wally's (pathetic, but still)—and she didn't expect she'd need any of them in the hour she'd be gone. She swiped open to her search engine to check the hours for the Greenport Historical Society:

Summer Hours 10 a.m.–1 p.m. Tuesday–Friday. Saturday 10–4.

Cruise to the Greenport Lighthouse Saturdays at 6 p.m.

SAVE THE LIGHTHOUSE! Fundraiser June 12

June twelfth was her deadline. The days were counting down. She needed answers. Maybe if she biked to the museum, she'd get some that could help her. What did she have to lose?

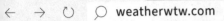

weatherwtw.com

Weather What to Wear Daily

Extended 10-Day forecast for Greenport, NY

June 5–13, 2025

As of 11:00 a.m. EDT

Small Craft Advisory +2 More*

Thursday, June 5

73 Degrees

>Considerable cloudiness. Occasional rain showers after midnight. Low 58°F. Winds ENE at 10–20 mph. Chance of rain 80%

Thursday, June 5: Rain/Wind

Friday, June 6: Rain/Wind

Saturday, June 7: Rain/Wind

Sunday, June 8: Rain/Wind

Monday, June 9: Rain/Wind

Tuesday, June 10: Rain/Wind

Wednesday, June 11: Rain/Wind

Thursday, June 12*: Rain/Wind

Friday, June 13*: Rain/Wind

Saturday, June 14th: Rain/Wind

>*First Blood Orange Moon in 200 years. Prepare for damaging winds, rains, and power outages. Secure crops and farm animals.

SEVEN

BENNY

PRESENT DAY

Greenport's marina was only twenty minutes away by bike. The sticky June heat made the ride unbearable, but the faster Benny pedaled, the more of a breeze she kicked up. There were no sidewalks in this town. Just rows and rows of grapevines (her own vineyard!), and farmland. By the time she made it into town, she was thirsty. She looked around, spotting one nautical-themed restaurant after another and lots of shops boasting clever names (like Vitamin Sea), an artisanal cheese store (whatever that was), that blue duck cookie shop her mom mentioned, a carousel, signs for a ferry to Shelter Island, and several stores selling tourist trap stuff like Greenport sweatshirts "on sale" for *seventy* dollars. She took several pictures, grabbed a water from a shop, and kept walking till she found the Greenport Historical Society, which was in a tiny old building on the waterfront. A bell on the door jingled when she stepped inside and found herself in a single-room museum where she was the only visitor.

"If you're looking for a restroom, you're out of luck. Ours isn't open to the public."

Benny turned around. A girl about her own age was sitting behind a counter of pathetic-looking souvenirs (stuffed dogs, museum pencils, and rubber bracelets that hadn't been in style since 2019). Her expression was unfriendly, her brown eyes holding a bit of a challenge to them (as if daring Benny to question this *no-restroom* validity). Above all, she looked bored. A plate of french fries swimming in ketchup sat in front of her, dangerously close to getting in her long curly brown hair. Benny took note of her vintage rock band T-shirt and the stack of bracelets that looked pretty on her wrist.

"Don't need a restroom," Benny said. "I was looking for a tour of the museum."

The girl blinked once. "It's one room. You're looking at it."

Someone really doesn't want to be here, Benny thought. She couldn't say she blamed the girl. It was the first week of summer vacation and this girl was stuck here instead of doing any number of things Benny had to assume girls with friends did in the summer. Benny wasn't the let's-sit-and-do-each-other's-nails type, but sometimes she thought it might be nice to have friends her own age.

"Zara!" An older woman wearing a red vest and a button that said *Greenport Historical Society* came bustling out of a back room. A cloud of floral perfume followed her. "Don't be rude to our guest. I'm sorry."

"Sorry, Grandma," Zara said, shoving a few french fries in her mouth so that the words came out like a mumble.

"Are you Thea Dabney?" Benny asked.

"Yes," said the woman pleasantly. "How can I help you?"

"Wally Ingram sent me. He thought you might be able to tell me some local history about a woman named Evelyn Terry."

Her eyes lit up. "Evelyn Terry! Founder of the inn, planter of Long Island's first grapevines, and the woman who single-handedly got our lighthouse built. You know," Thea said, moving closer, "she was a trailblazer for her time. Women in the 1800s always took their husband's name when they married, but Evelyn insisted on keeping her own so that the Terry line could live on."

"I didn't even think of that," Benny realized.

Zara cleared her throat. "Shouldn't she pay the museum fee before you start spilling facts?"

"Zara!" her grandmother admonished.

"It's alright." Benny fished in her pocket for a ten-dollar bill she wasn't ready to part with. "How much is the entry fee?"

"There isn't one." Thea glared at her granddaughter. "But we're always happy to accept donations."

Benny reached in her pocket again, pulled out two dollar bills, and crammed them in a tin can that had been wrapped with a picture and the words SAVE THE LIGHTHOUSE!

"Thank you! We're happy to give you a tour, aren't we Zara? Especially if we want to earn money this summer to have 'a life,' as you call it while staying with your grandmother?"

Clearly there was a story there.

Zara jumped off the chair she was sitting on and pushed the french fries aside. She stepped out from behind the counter revealing cutoff jean shorts and beat-up unlaced sneakers. "Fine. Let's go on the 'tour.'" She used air quotes and Benny tried not to laugh.

Zara pulled an index card out from her pocket and started reading it in a bored voice. "Welcome to the Greenport Historical Society, home of the largest collection of Greenport artifacts on Long Island. As if Greenport artifacts would be anywhere else."

Her grandmother coughed.

Zara pointed to a large brass contraption. "Behold the wonder of the once-functioning oil lamp from the Greenport Lighthouse, a historical artifact we're hoping to preserve for future generations."

She noticed Thea was mouthing the words Zara was reciting.

"Be a part of the renovation!" Zara added with mock enthusiasm. "Our fundraising gala is June twelfth, and tickets are still available."

June twelfth. "Is there a reason you all chose that date? Does it mean something to the lighthouse? Or Greenport? Or is it a date from local history?" Benny pressed.

Zara blinked. "Nope. It's just your average Thursday."

Bummer. Benny deflated. She caught Zara staring at her and tried to perk up. "Are there any cool artifacts in the museum I should check out?"

Zara took a deep breath. "In our loft area, you will find paintings done by local artists as far back as 1825, including some by Evelyn Terry. You will also learn how the Rudd family turned a small town into a destination, thanks to their factory and thriving fishing port. They still own everything in this place," Zara said. "*Anyway,* Long Island has a long history of being the fishing capital of the East Coast. In recent years, menhaden, more commonly known as bunker fish, have returned to the island after disappearing from overfishing. It was the abundance of fishing that drew Long Island to put a lighthouse in its waters and—"

Benny cut her off. "The fish story is fascinating, but I'm really interested in learning more about Evelyn Terry. Do you have any information on her? Can you show me which paintings she did?"

Thea stepped forward. "She did a few of ships in storms, and this one, here, was always popular, even though it's of a pirate ship, and pirates were before her time."

Benny stared at the small watercolor of a ship with a black flag bearing a skull and crossbones. A figurehead hung from the front of the ship. The ship was just like the one she wrote about in her journal. "May I take a picture?" Benny asked.

"Of course," Thea said, fiddling with a gold mermaid broach on her silk top.

"Is there anything else you can tell me about her?" Benny tried. "I'm told she was a big reader. Would you happen to know anything about her interests?" *Her book interests?*

Zara folded her arms across her chest. "Are you doing a summer reading project on the woman or something?"

A pit formed in her stomach. *Why do you want to know?* "Or something," Benny told her.

"I'm sorry, I don't, but I can do some digging in the

archives," Thea offered. "Why don't you come back next week, and I'll see if I can find anything?"

I can't wait that long. "Thank you," she said anyway and watched Thea walk away, talking quietly with Zara. *Think, Benny. If Evelyn painted ships in storms and pirate ships, could there be a book out there about either of those things? Maybe.* Her hand brushed her pocket where Evelyn's letter and journal pages were hidden. She was too nervous to let the pages out of her sight. *What am I missing?* Benny exhaled, feeling her shoulders clench from frustration. There was nothing at the museum that could help her. What a waste of time.

Downstairs, the bell jingled, and she heard Thea go through the whole speech instead of Zara this time. Benny pulled the letter out and started to reread it again.

Someone yanked the pages from her hands.

"Hey!" Benny protested, whirling around to find Zara holding Evelyn's letter. Her heart pounded in her chest. *Don't read that. Don't read that!*

"Stealing from a museum?" Zara hissed, holding it above her head. "Are you out of your mind? My grandmother will have your head."

Benny swiped the air to get it back, afraid to rip the old paper in the process. "I didn't steal it! It's mine." She knew she sounded angry, but she didn't care. This wasn't a game. Well, it was a game, but it was *her* game. This girl had no part in it. "Read who the letter is addressed to, Everly Benedict. That's me. I can even recite the letter if you don't believe me."

Zara lowered the letter in her hand and read it fast.

"See? Hand it over," Benny said, trying not to sound panicked. She didn't know Zara. What if she told people what Benny was doing? What if someone tried to steal the game out from under her?

"Zara? Everything okay?" her grandmother called up to them. "Telling our guest everything you know?"

"Yes, Grandma," Zara yelled. "She's having the time of her life." Zara handed her back the letter. "So you're her."

"Her?" Benny repeated, taking the letter and folding it carefully before placing it back in her pocket. She was already cursing herself for taking it out in public.

"Evelyn's heir," Zara said, her voice lower.

Benny tensed. "You know about the game?"

"I think I can help you. Are you hungry?" Zara headed to the steps. "I know a great place for lunch."

"It's ten forty-five." Benny said. "And I don't really have time to—"

Zara ignored her and kept walking. "Good. We'll be the first ones there."

EIGHT

BENNY

PRESENT DAY

"Is it ever going to stop raining?" Zara looked up at the sky in annoyance as she led Benny outside and past the docks using a "shortcut," as she called it, to the restaurant. Outside, it was misting. Again. "If I'm stuck here all summer in that museum and it rains every day, I will—"

Benny cut her off. "You said you could help me. How?" She wasn't in the habit of following orders from someone she didn't know, but if Zara knew something about Evelyn that could help her with the game, she had to find out what it was.

"Let's eat first." Zara was equally good at being evasive. "Crabby Carrie's will be open by eleven, and Ryan is on today, so we can eat for free. He owes me." Zara started walking, and Benny had no choice but to follow.

"So that's your grandma at the museum?" Benny asked, trying to fill the silence.

"Yep. I'm staying with her all summer while my parents are away on sabbatical researching, of all things, pirate lore in Trinidad, and Tobago and the British Virgin Islands. My dad is from Trinidad, and he's always been fascinated with this story he heard as a kid about some cursed pirate treasure that was lost in the 1600s. Anyway, they get two months of turquoise waters and sandy white beaches, and I get to stay here. On exciting Long Island," Zara deadpanned.

"You didn't want to go with them?" Benny asked.

"Said I'd be bored and they'd be busy doing research and traveling from island to island." Zara stared out at the water, visible from the path through town. "I love my grandma, but with my parents away, and my sister doing this whole back-packing across Europe college thing, it's just the two of us. And she goes to bed at eight-thirty so she thinks I should too." She exhaled slowly. "Sorry. I won't bore you with my drama."

"Bore away," Benny said, warming up. When was the last time she'd had an actual conversation with someone her own age? "It's kind of nice to hear someone else's drama instead of dealing with my own."

Zara offered a hint of a smile. "The best cure for drama? Crab legs. Come on."

The town was so small, it only took five minutes to walk back the way Benny originally came by bike and reach the docks.

As they passed a fancy restaurant named Hooked, a small bell rang over the door, and an older woman stepped outside. Benny noticed she was wearing a sweater, pants, and pearls in June, an expensive handbag draped over one pale arm. A cloud of perfume followed her. The scent was pleasant—a hint of gardenia and vanilla intermingling. She gave Zara a cool smile, her gray eyes flitting to Benny's for a half a second. Zara stopped short and grasped Benny's arm to make her do the same.

"Good morning, Mrs. Rudd," Zara said, sounding more polite than Benny had heard her all morning.

Rudd. Benny felt herself inhale sharply. She tried not to register emotion on her face.

"Ms. Dabney, hello," the woman said coolly. "How are things at the historical society?"

"Fine, thank you," Zara said. "Grandma is happy you're able to join us for the lighthouse gala."

"So much history there, dear, how could a Rudd not be in attendance?" Her eyes took in Benny with interest. "You haven't introduced me to your friend."

Zara faltered. "Oh, yeah, sorry, this is—"

Benny cut her off. "Benny," she said quickly, not revealing her given name. "My name is Benny."

Mrs. Rudd's plum-stained lips curled ever so slightly into a frown. "Benny," she repeated slowly. "Welcome to Greenport."

"Thank you," Benny said politely.

Mrs. Rudd took out her umbrella. "Enjoy the day, girls, before it rains."

She headed off down the street, and Benny heard Zara exhale.

"That is Vivian Rudd, mayor of this town, the wealthiest woman alive and possibly the scariest," Zara said. "You don't want to cross her."

"No, I don't," Benny said softly. *I'm not letting her take Evelyn's inheritance.*

"Let's go," Zara said, motioning in the opposite direction. "We're almost at the restaurant. Ours is nowhere as fancy as this one."

Zara led her to the entrance of an outdoor place on the docks, with a crooked hand-painted sign: *Crabby Carrie's.* Benny hoped she could get something to eat with the ten dollars in her pocket. A boy around their own age came to the entrance, holding a tray of paper plates and cups.

"Sorry. We're not open till—" When he saw Zara and

Benny, he almost dropped his tray. "No. No. No, we had a deal, Zara. Mondays and Wednesdays only, when Carrie isn't here," the boy said, placing the tray on a nearby table. "And just you. You can't bring a guest." He eyed Benny suspiciously.

His fair-skinned nose was peeling from what looked like a bad early-summer sunburn, and he had reddish-blond hair. He wore a blue tee with a Hawaiian print shirt under a green Crabby Carrie's apron. His cargo shorts were frayed at the hem, and he was wearing flip-flops. His face was flushed, and a curl brushing across his brown eyes looked damp from the summer humidity.

Zara folded her arms across her chest. "The rules of our agreement have changed. We're both eating for free today, and we want king crab legs."

The boy groaned. "How am I supposed to get two orders from the kitchen without an order slip?"

Zara kept her expression neutral. "I don't know. That's your problem."

"Come on. It's the first week, and you've eaten like two pounds of crab legs already."

Zara grinned wickedly. "Think of how many I'll have eaten by end of August."

The boy ran his hands through his hair.

"Am I missing something?" Benny asked, curious.

"This is Ryan," Zara said, "and he owes me from now till forever because it's his fault I failed a science project worth ten percent of our final grade."

"She's being dramatic," Ryan said weakly, and Benny knew Zara had his number. "She had like a hundred average in the class."

"And because of you, my average got messed up," Zara said, getting agitated.

"You still had an A...didn't you?" he squeaked.

Zara's nostrils flared. "That's not the point. I was going for a perfect score in science while I served as class treasurer and had track and was competing for state. Something you wouldn't understand since your idea of a school activity is Frisbee in the park."

He swallowed hard. "What's wrong with Frisbee?"

"My point is, our project was going great, lab partner, till you went rogue." Zara was yelling now. "And now Mr. Keating has to spend the summer without eyebrows!" Ryan pulled at the collar of his T-shirt.

"Someone lost their eyebrows?" Benny asked, intrigued.

"For our project, Ryan accidentally grabbed sodium metal and dropped it in water," Zara said.

"I wasn't wearing my contacts," Ryan squeaked. "I misread the bottle. Innocent mistake."

"Innocent? The sodium metal released hydrogen gas, which got so hot, it burst into flames!" Zara said. "And the sparks hit the wood table we were standing at and set the whole table on fire, and Mr. Keating came running, and the explosion burnt off his eyebrows."

Ryan turned desperately to Benny. "Eyebrows grow back. And besides, it was a tiny fire. This is what fire extinguishers are for."

"My point is, our bad grade is all Ryan's fault." Her eyes were like slits. "Which is why he has to give me free lunch at Crabby Carrie's any time I want this summer."

"Yes, *you*, but I didn't say you could bring a friend!" Ryan argued.

"I'm changing the rules. Ryan, say hi to Everly Benedict. She'd like crab legs too."

Ryan's expression faltered. "Everly Benedict? You're her? You're the heir?"

Benny froze.

"Wait. You know she's an heir too?" Zara asked him.

"How do *you* know?" he countered.

"I read her letter," Zara said.

"*Stole* my letter," Benny clarified. "And I prefer to go by Benny, if it's all the same."

"I gave it back," Zara pointed out. "Honestly, I don't even

know what this heir business is about. I just said I did to get out
of the museum. If I had to sit in that room for another hour..."

"So you can't help me?" Benny realized, disappointed.

"Help? What kind of help?" Ryan interrupted.

"No, sorry," Zara confessed. "But I do—"

"I'm going to go." Benny cut her off. This is what she got
for trying to trust people.

"No, wait," Zara said. "Have crab legs with me."

"No crab legs!" Ryan argued.

Zara ignored him. "I'm sorry, okay," she said, her voice
softer than it had been all morning. "I am the granddaughter
of a local history buff. I'm sure I can help you." She brightened.
"And since it's history, my grandmother might even count it as
work hours. You're trying to figure out that riddle, right?"

Benny felt the knot in her stomach tighten. "Who said it
was a riddle?"

Ryan blocked her path off the dock. "Stay. She may not be
able to help you, but I can."

"Oh really, how can you help?" Benny couldn't help but
sound skeptical.

"Yeah, you, Ryan? How?" Zara seconded.

Ryan's brown eyes found Benny's, and there was something desperate in them Benny couldn't quite read. "Because I
know why Evelyn Terry gave you the deadline of June twelfth."

ENTRY 4

From Evelyn Terry's Private Journal,
Dated June 5, 1825

Last night I tossed and turned like
a ship in a storm, unable to stop
thinking about Captain Jonas Kimble,
Aggy's warning, and things I didn't
understand...

I awoke to the sound of my curtains flapping in the wind and
looked out my window onto our fields. It wasn't raining, but
the clouds were a mixture of dark and light, as if they were
fighting to see which would win out. Father had taught me to
read the weather to try to determine if a storm was coming or

would pass us by, but the clouds this morning stuck to the sky like toffee. Father had to think rain would hold off long enough for my brothers to finish their work. I could already see them in the field. Downstairs, I could hear Mama beginning her day, rising with the sun. I had chores to do too, and then school.

But Aggy's cryptic words gnawed at me. Why had we been the only two to see Kimble or his ship? Why did she want me to keep quiet about what we saw? *People won't understand*, she'd said about our friends. *Our friends will in time, but if you try to tell them now, it will only frighten them about what comes next.*

What comes next?

I didn't have the gift of sight like Aggy, but I needed to understand what this man's arrival meant for all of us. And I wasn't sure Aggy would tell me.

That's why, an hour later, after rushing through feeding the animals, I ran down the path, cut through the brush, and made my way to the island.

The sky still threatened to rain, and the fog this morning was so thick on the shore, it made it hard to see, but I knew the island was out there. I removed my shoes and stepped onto the sand. The fog seemed to part, making a path visible to the sandbar for me to walk across. Hair stood up on the back of my neck. Was I being watched? I looked around and saw no one, so I ran across, the mist so thick around me, it felt like it might swallow me whole. I could hear the island singing, like a song. *Evelyn Terry. Welcome!*

The second I hit the opposite shore, the clouds parted, and the sun peeked through, radiant and warm, casting a glow on the water that seemed to turn from deep blue to aquamarine before my very eyes. I could hear the waterfall at one end of the beach, which fed right into the water. I knew the cave was there—the only place on the island we never dared explore because it was so dark and cold. Instead, I longed to stretch out on the sand and stare out at the nothingness before me. It always surprised me how Greenport wasn't even a fleck of dust in the distance when I was here, and I never saw boats or other people. It was just me. On a private island I'd found. I never questioned it.

But today was different. I could sense him nearby.

Captain Kimble was here.

I started walking down the beach to find him, and the island seemed to stretch and grow in response, the sand going on forever. For a while, I thought I was lost. That maybe I circled the same spot twice, but I hadn't seen the waterfall again. Instead, I stumbled upon the fort, growing up out of the trees, covered partially in vines that parted for me as I approached.

Was this a mirage? Where had this fortress come from? It was crumbling—or maybe only half-built, with a single cannon at the ready if someone were to attack. The fort looked like it was practically taken back by the land, the bricks covered in moss, sand littering the floor, the windows' shutters hanging off. The sea air, as Mama was always telling me, weathered everything. But the closer I got, the wider my eyes became. The fort looked lived-in. Through the open shutters, I could see a table set with candles burning, a fireplace, and thick bedding on a bed, a small table and chairs with a bountiful basket of ripe fruit waiting to be eaten. And there, lying on a long couch, with a wide-brimmed tricorn leather hat covering his eyes, was Kimble.

"Are you going to stand there, kid?" I heard him say. "Or is there something you wanted?"

I tried not to act startled, but I was. "How did you know I was here?"

"I could hear you breathing before you even reached the beach. I thought I told you to keep off the island, poppet."

Poppet? "I'm...not a good listener," I admitted.

"I can see that."

"Well, you can't actually *see* anything as your hat is covering your eyes," I noted.

He sighed heavily and sat up, removing his hat to look at me. His blue eyes looked even bluer in the glare of the sun shining through cracks in the fort. "I don't have time for debates, kid. You shouldn't be here. Now be a good girl, and go home and play with dolls or help your mother or something."

I took offense to that. "I don't play with dolls," I said. "I'm practically a grown-up."

He scoffed.

"I brought you food, thinking you'd be hungry, but if you don't want it, I'll take it with me." Food, I'd learned with my older brothers, was a good motivator.

"What did you bring?" he asked, standing up now and coming straight for the sack in my hands. "Say it's warm bread, and you can stay for a spell. I haven't had warm food in, well, however long it's been since I lost my last crew."

"It's warm bread," I said as he yanked the sack from my hands. His manners were poor. He didn't even say thank you. "And what do you mean *lost*?"

He sat down at the table and didn't bother to use his pocketknife to cut off a piece. He just dug into the loaf with his teeth, sounding blissful as he chewed. "This is good. You make this?"

"Yes, and I asked you a question, sir."

"Sir?" He looked at me then, his head cocked in surprise. "No one has ever called me *sir* before. *Sir*?" he said, trying it on for size. "No, I'm not sure it suits me." He took another hunk of bread in his mouth and chewed some more. "The name is Kimble. And you are?"

"I'm not sure I want you to know my name," I said stiffly, and he looked amused. "But if you must know, my friends call me Sparrow."

"*Sparrow* will do." He looked at me. "And to answer your question, *Sparrow*, when I say *lost*, I mean my crew is gone." He made a cutting motion across his neck, and I paled. "Deceased. Dead. No one lasts long around me. Not with this noose around my neck."

"I see no noose."

"It's an expression, Sparrow." He reached in the sack to see what else was there and found the apple. He tossed it back to me. "You can keep this. The island has plenty of fruit. And I don't plan on being stuck here long."

"Stuck? How could anyone feel stuck in this paradise?" I questioned.

He wagged a finger at me. "Aah, see, that's how the island gets you. Pulls you in. Makes you feel all safe and warm. It invites you. Welcomes you. Calling your name like you're a king or, in your case, queen."

I froze. I'd heard the island calling to me several times.

"When really all this place wants to do is *BAM*!" He slammed a hand on the table, and a coconut rolled off. "Tricks you and curses you, like it did me."

"I think the one doing the tricking is you, *sir—Kimble*," I said correcting myself. "That can't really be your name, can it? Jonas Kimble?"

He placed the cocked hat back on his head and looked at me. "It's my name, all right. Heard it before?" he asked with a smirk. "I'm famous in these parts."

"*Infamous* is more like it, and it can't be your name. It belongs to a pirate in the 1600s," I said, my hands starting to shake. I held my breath, waiting for a response I wasn't sure I wanted to hear.

He walked over to me then and crossed his arms, the smirk on his face widening. "What makes you think I'm not him, Sparrow? You'll believe in a beautiful island appearing out of nowhere and inviting you on, but you can't believe the young man standing in front of you is a two-hundred-year-old pirate?" He put his hat squarely back on his head. "And I prefer the term *marauder*, thank you very much."

Every bone in my body knew then he was telling the truth. A pirate, who should be dead and buried more than a century ago, stood before me as a young man. This island, which had appeared only to me and my friends in the last few weeks, which Papa didn't believe existed, was otherworldly, like Kimble. And there had to be a reason both were here. "What do you want?" I asked.

"What do I want?" he said, his voice raised slightly. "To

finally be cut loose. A free man. Rid of this shackle and the blasted treasure." He motioned to the chest in the corner of the room, which I hadn't noticed till now. My eyes must have widened then because he made a point to get in my face. "Oh, don't be swayed by what's in here, poppet. It's a trap. Poison, pure and simple." His face, so calm and sure, crumpled for a moment. "It will take everyone you love and destroy them and you. You don't want to be near this chest. You don't even want a coin, because once you have a taste, you're hooked." He looked at me, his voice quieter, as if he was in a trance. "It sounds fine at first. Never aging. But then you remember, you stay the same while others grow old. You're cursed to watch everyone around you die. To be helpless as the world passes you by. I know that now. I knew it 150 years ago, but I had to wait to get the treasure back to this blasted place. That's my curse—having the agonizing wait for the next Blood Orange Moon to change my fate. So I'm back!" His smile was maniacal. "I may have lost her, lost my crew, but I made it to this blasted place once more to give back what I took. All that's left to do is find that one final piece, and I'll be free."

"Final piece?" I whispered. "What do you mean?"

"Sparrow!"

Kimble and I looked at each other.

"That's my best friend, Aggy. She's looking for me," I said

as I heard a small meow and looked down at the orange and white tabby cat that appeared. She was a one-eyed cat, with one side of her face in a permanent squint.

Kimble seemed to take a step back. "What is that thing?"

I scooped the kitten up. "Aggy's cat. We call her Winks because she only has one eye," I said, letting the cat purr in my arms.

"Well, take Winks and go on now," he said, shooing me away.

"But you didn't finish—" I started to protest.

"Seriously, kid. Get out of here. While the island still gives you a chance to leave." He slammed the fort door behind me, and I watched as the vines seemed to shift and grow in front of the door, making the entrance that was there a moment ago, disappear.

NINE

BENNY

"You know why my deadline is June twelfth? *Really*?" Benny stared Ryan down. Was he bluffing or telling the truth? While she'd taken to Zara a bit too easily, there was something about Ryan that made her put her guard up. Benny didn't want to reveal her cards or show too much interest. She knew how to play the game. Knew when to speak and when to be quiet.

"You have to find the missing island by June twelfth, or Evelyn's game is over," Ryan said with confidence.

Benny rolled her eyes. "Tell me something I don't know." She grabbed her bag.

Zara blocked her path. "I'm sorry, did he just say 'missing island'? How can an island go missing?"

Benny and Ryan looked at each other and she wondered if he knew any more than she did. She had to be careful with her next words. "It can't."

"If you believe that, then you'll never find it," Ryan told her, his voice even. "But you must want to. Otherwise, why would you visit the museum? You're looking for intel on Evelyn, aren't you? She left you riddles, right?"

"A riddle. In her letter," Zara said knowingly.

Ryan's eyes widened. "What's the riddle?"

Benny wasn't sure she wanted either of these people knowing. She didn't know them. Which meant she didn't trust them, even if she was starting to warm up to Zara. Evelyn had entrusted this game to her, and she was meant to play it alone. Wasn't she? *You were going to partner with Mom*, a small voice in her head said. *She's family.*

"Tell me the riddle; I'll tell you why you have a deadline of June twelfth," Ryan said, his eyes challenging.

She knew the look well. Benny folded her arms and waited. Benny had learned a long time ago that people liked to hear themselves talk. When she made them uncomfortable with silence, they tended to spill more and give her what she wanted. Whether it was an extension of the rent due date or an ice cream cone when she was twenty cents short. Ryan was no exception. "Tell me why the dead-line is June twelfth, and *then* I'll decide if I want to tell you the clue," she volleyed back.

"Ooh. This is getting good." Zara sat down and put her hands under her chin.

"Fine," he groaned. "June twelfth is the date of the next Blood Orange Moon."

Benny froze.

Zara started laughing. "The Blood Orange *what*?"

"Blood Orange Moon," he repeated, his expression seri-ous now. "There hasn't been one in two hundred years, and the next one is due June twelfth."

"How do you know?" Benny whispered, her heart beating faster. Evelyn's journal pages mentioned this Blood Orange Moon. Why didn't she think to google whether it was a real thing? She just assumed Evelyn was referring to a full moon or some sort of made-up storm nickname.

"A Blood Orange Moon is when a lunar eclipse, a second full moon in one calendar month, and an orange moon, which is when the sun and moon appear in the sky at the same time, all happen on the same night," Ryan explained. "And the next one is June twelfth."

"That's a weird coincidence, no?" Zara asked.

Very weird, Benny thought but didn't want to say. "This moon—was there superstitions around it in the 1800s?"

"Oh yeah." Ryan nodded. "Farmers thought it was a bad omen. Said they were cursed."

Cursed. Evelyn mentioned a curse in her letter.

Ryan motioned to the sky. "Traditionally Blood Orange Moons usher in a lot of rain and bad weather, ruin crops, cause strange events...if you believe almanacs. And for some reason, Evelyn Terry wants you to find her island by that specific date. I don't think it *is* a coincidence, but I'd have to read your letter to know for sure."

It wasn't a coincidence. Benny could see that now. But she was in over her head here. Did she trust these two to tell them more? Zara had already read the riddle. Why was she hesitating with Ryan? *You're being paranoid* she told herself. *You have to learn to trust people.* She made a snap decision. She pulled out the letter. Her heart was beating fast. Ryan's eyes widened as he looked at the faded page in Benny's hands. "I'm taking a break!" he called back to the kitchen. "May I?" he asked, nodding to the paper. Benny held it out to him. Carefully, he took the note and read it fast. With the wind picking up, the paper flapped in his hand and Benny prayed he was holding on tight. He handed it back to her and looked at her strangely. "Carrie? Can we get three orders of crab legs? We're going to be here a while."

Ten minutes later, after Ryan had a heated conversation with the woman behind the counter, who it turned out was his aunt and *the* Crabby Carrie (the name fit), the three of them were sitting at a table near the water, and Benny was eating the freshest seafood she'd ever had. And the first crab legs she'd ever eaten. Not that she was telling them that. The other two didn't notice how hard it was for her to use the tool to crack the legs open. They both had on bibs and fingers full of butter. The food had sated her and she was starting to feel more comfortable around both of them.

"So let me get this straight," Zara said, cracking open another leg and pulling out the crabmeat. "Evelyn wants you to find an island that doesn't exist, and if you do, you inherit her fortune?"

"Yes, but...no?" Benny said carefully. "She must have believed the island existed, or why else would she leave her whole inheritance to me? So I have to believe it's out there too."

"She's got a point," Ryan said to Zara. "If she loses, the Rudds get everything." He turned to Benny. "Sorry, my dad is on the board, so that part I knew. He's been showing your mom around."

"Your dad is Harris?" Benny said in surprise.

Ryan nodded. "He didn't mention me, did he? Probably talked about my little sister though, right? She lives with my stepmom. Or is that ex-stepmom since they just got divorced? We only get to see her every other weekend now so mostly it's just him and me," Ryan said miserably and leaned back in his chair. He would have fallen off if she and Zara hadn't righted it at the same time. A look flickered across his face she couldn't read. "We have zero in common except Evelyn Terry's game." He bit his lip. "He doesn't want you to lose. Bad for his businesses so maybe if I help you find the island..." Ryan drummed his fingers on the table. "...he'll remember I exist."

Benny tensed. Was Harris a jerk? He seemed so nice whenever Benny saw him, and he treated her mom well, which sounded like the opposite way he treated his kid. "That bites." Ryan nodded.

"Before you go letting Ryan help you, don't forget," Zara butted in. "I'm the one with a grandmother who is a walking, talking Greenport history book. I may have never heard about this orange moon thing, but I know stuff."

"Just not science stuff," Ryan mumbled.

Zara brandished her seafood cracker at his nose. "My grams has lots of old papers, journals. She has one from a girl who supposedly went looking for Captain Jonas Kimble's treasure. Said it was like a fountain of youth. That it could heal her."

Benny felt the hair on her arms stand up. *Treasure? Fountain of youth?*

Ryan started to laugh. "A pirate treasure? In Greenport?" He gave Benny a look. "People have looked for Kimble's treasure for years and never found it. Nothing is here."

"You say that because it hasn't been found," Zara argued. "Doesn't mean it's not out there."

"It's just hearsay," Ryan told her. "Just a reason to have a pirate festival every July."

"Festival or not, Kimble is still a legend in these parts," Zara said passionately. "Right up there with Blackbeard and Captain Kidd. His ship, the *Kraken*, was supposedly stolen from the British army, had twenty cannons, was the fastest in the sea, and could carry two hundred tons."

Benny had goose bumps, but maybe that was from the wind picking up on the water. Dark clouds were rolling in again, and it looked like more rain was coming. At the same time, she could feel the tension in her shoulders unclenching. It felt good to talk about the game. Here were two people her own age who seemed actually interested and—was she wrong here?—wanted to help her. But should she let them? Or do it on her own like she did everything else? She was so conflicted. "So you believe the treasure really is buried somewhere out here?"

"My parents do, so yeah." Zara nodded. "They think he stole his biggest treasure from his love, who was also a pirate by the name of Grace O'Malley. And in a classic pirate move, she stole that treasure from an actual queen in the British Virgin Islands." Zara dipped a crab leg in butter. "That's part of the reason why they're there this summer. Apparently that treasure was cursed." Zara shrugged. "If you believe the legend."

"That's what they say about Blood Orange Moons—they're cursed," Ryan added, just as a large gust of wind threatened to blow several tablecloths off the tables.

Benny didn't believe in curses. Luck, yes. Curses, no. Then again, she was currently searching for an island that didn't seem to exist. Maybe she shouldn't be so narrow-minded. But if there was a treasure, and it was cursed, and on this missing island...why did Evelyn want Benny to find it?

Benny tapped her buttery fingers on the paper tablecloth making grease stains. *Treasure.* The fact it was mentioned in the first riddle couldn't be a coincidence. Evelyn knew what a Blood Orange Moon was, and that one was coming, which is why she gave Benny the deadline. *Could she really have thought that far ahead?* she asked herself. She needed to get ahold of more pages from Evelyn's journal, but to do that, she'd have to figure out this riddle and find the books.

But did she have to go it alone? *It's okay to ask for help sometimes, Guppy,* she could hear Grams say. Her back was up against the wall, and she had a deadline. Ryan and Zara were local and knew town history. Was it against the rules of the game to ask for help?

"Alright," Benny said, the words feeling foreign on her tongue. "If you two are free, maybe I could use some help."

"Yes!" Ryan crowed, a bit too enthusiastically, and butter sloshed out of the cups and onto the table.

"I'm in," Zara said. "I even think I can figure out what book or books you're looking for. It needs to be published during Evelyn's time, right?"

"And it's one of her favorite books?" Ryan asked.

"Yes, but her house has hundreds of books. Thousands! And I've tried all the classics," Benny said miserably. "*David Copperfield, Jane Eyre, Wuthering Heights...*"

"But did you look for a book about pirate treasure?" Zara challenged.

"No," Benny realized and pulled out her phone, quickly googling the words, *books 1800s pirates treasure*. She gasped. "Oh my god." She looked at Zara. *Treasure Island* was written in 1883!

They looked at one another.

Zara stood up fast and grabbed Ryan by the arm. "Let's go find that book."

GREENPORT HERALD

June 13, 1825

WEARY GREENPORT RECOVERS FROM BLOOD ORANGE MOON

BY JAKE BATTERON

The people of Greenport are recovering today from a celestial moon event referred to in the Farmers' Annual as the Blood Orange Moon. The rare occurrence, said to only happen once every two hundred years, caused heavy rain and flooding. Ernest Cooper's corn crop was destroyed, ruining his prospects for the upcoming harvest season. Ashley Ford says the wind was so fierce, a tree took out her barn, spooking several horses that have yet to be recovered. Please alert the Fords if any colts are spotted.

Elias Rudd is asking Greenport to be on the lookout for his son Axel Rudd, who disappeared last night during the storm. Anyone who knows of Axel Rudd's whereabouts may call on Elias Rudd immediately. The Henderson family is also searching for their daughter Laurel, who stepped out to get some air before the weather turned.

As the Blood Orange Moon comes on the heels of a Cough outbreak, it is important to note there has been much confusion, and no word has come yet from many households that may be affected by storm or illness. The Cough has shut down the new Greenport School House for almost a week. Elias Rudd says the Greenport Mercantile will remain closed for the foreseeable future.

TEN

BENNY

PRESENT DAY

Zara and Ryan both had bikes that were locked up at the nearby bike rack by the dock. New ones. Ryan's was a fancy neon orange mountain bike and Zara's was a mint green with one of those baskets on the front. Benny was just thinking how not Zara's type the bike was when Zara blurted out: "It's my sister's. Mine was stuck behind the lawn mower, and I couldn't get it out."

"Just hurry up and get it unlocked," Ryan said, already seated on his bike seat and bouncing up and down. "I hate being down here."

"On the docks?" Benny asked, looking around. While the large yachts and bigger boats had been docked near Crabby

Carrie's, this dock had older vessels. There was a peeling fishing boat moored at the end of the short dock, a white ferry that said *Southhold Historical Society Lighthouse Tours* on one side, and a few smaller recreational boats. "Why?"

"He's afraid of the Crab," Zara said, smirking.

"Am not," Ryan said, his eyes scanning the dock for what Benny could only assume was a giant mutant sea crab. "You don't see him, do you?"

"The Crab is a person?" Benny questioned, holding her bike steady as another wind gust threatened to blow them off the dock. The wind had only gotten fiercer since they left the restaurant, and dark clouds were drawing closer. If they didn't hurry, they'd get soaked on the ride back to the house.

Benny felt something wind around her legs and jumped. She laughed when she realized it was an orange tabby cat. It cuddled up to her and wouldn't leave, purring as it sat on her feet. "Hello, there," she said, bending down to pet the cat, who let her. She started to scratch behind the cat's ear and realized the cat only had one eye; its other eye was shut tight.

"He's just a fisherman everyone calls the Crab because he's so cranky," Zara said, getting her bike out and motioning to the fishing boat at the end of the dock. "He lives on his boat and hates when anyone loiters near it. Especially kids."

"He yells," Ryan told Benny, his brown eyes crinkling with worry. "Never go near his cat."

"Oh!" Benny stood up, and the cat stayed, sitting on the top of her shoes and licking its paws as if it had nowhere to be. Benny carefully pulled out her camera and took a picture of the feline. "This cat seems to want company."

"That may be, but he'll think you're trying to steal it," Ryan said solemnly. "I've had it happen. Like anyone would want a one-eyed cat."

"WINKS!" someone yelled. "Winks! Where are you?" At the end of the dock, a young man in his thirties, dirty blond hair, with stubble, wearing a ripped T-shirt and a pair of jeans, stood barefoot on the deck of the fishing boat. He saw Benny staring and glowered in response.

"There is the Crab now. Step away from his cat. Move, move, move," Ryan panicked, grabbing his bike, jumping on, and pedaling away, his motion unstable.

The cat trotted toward the boat, and the man jumped onto the dock like an agile cat himself. Benny noted it had to be a three-feet drop. She watched as he picked up the cat and started cooing at it. She snuck a picture of him and the boat too, for no other reason than it was funny to see a grown man talking baby talk to an animal.

"Ryan's a bit dramatic, but Ansel is a grump," Zara said,

watching as the man climbed back onto the boat with the cat in tow. "I think that's his name. His grandfather and dad were the same way, according to my grandma," Zara said, starting to walk her bike off the dock. "I think he's the third guy to own the boat, and he rarely leaves it. Kind of young to be a hermit."

Yes, Benny thought, watching the fisherman disappear.

A low rumble of thunder sounded in the distance. They needed to get going.

"You two coming or not?" Ryan yelled from the safety of the land.

Benny and Zara ran their bikes down the dock, and then Benny led the way home.

ELEVEN

BENNY

PRESENT DAY

The rain was just starting to fall in big fat drops as the three bikes reached the gravel path at Evelyn's estate. Benny figured Wally must have seen her riding up with Zara and Ryan because like magic, one of the garage doors opened, allowing them to park their bikes inside. Thunder rumbled in the distance as Zara and Ryan followed Benny into the house from an entrance in the garage.

"Wow. Wow. Wow," Ryan said as he looked around. "I haven't been here in forever, but this place is as nice as I remember." He looked wistful. "I can't believe it's yours."

"Temporarily," Benny stressed, glancing at the TV that was on in the living room. News 12, a local channel, was on, and the meteorologist was showing the seven-day forecast: All rain. Something about a low-pressure system that was just hovering over the east end of the island. "It all depends on whether I beat Evelyn's game."

"Then what are we waiting for?" Zara walked to a bookshelf in the kitchen and started pulling cookbooks off it. "Let's find those books."

"I see we have guests," said Wally, appearing in the doorway with a plate of chocolate chip cookies as if he knew Benny wouldn't come back alone.

"This is Zara and Ryan," Benny explained. "They came back to help me find a book that is part of Evelyn's riddle."

"I suspected you'd find reinforcement troops in town," Wally noted. "Would anyone like a freshly baked cookie?"

No one said no to that offer.

"Do these have cinnamon?" Ryan asked, munching away. "I feel like I taste cinnamon."

"A hint of cinnamon, yes," Wally said, amused.

"Do you know if you've seen a copy of *Treasure Island* anywhere in the house?" Benny asked Wally hopefully, still tasting the warm chocolate on her tongue. "An old copy?"

"*Treasure Island*, you say?" Wally asked. "There isn't a copy in the library?"

"I don't remember seeing one," Benny said, cursing herself for not keeping a list of book titles.

Wally thought for a moment. "Hmm...I must admit, sometimes books walk off with guests."

The thought made Benny's heart seize with terror. She hadn't thought of that before. The house was rented to vacationers. What if someone already had the book? *No, it's here*, her gut told her. "But there's a chance it would be in the library, and I missed it, right?"

"I believe there's a chance, yes," Wally confirmed with a gentle smile.

"Lets go find it!" Benny ran down the hall. "Everyone, follow me. Not you, Wally!" she yelled back. "Unless you want to!"

"Waiting on something in the oven, dear. Good luck!" he called back.

"I'll just take the cookies with us," she heard Zara say as she and Ryan followed her down the hall to the library.

There was a flash of lightning followed by a gust of wind that made the windows rattle.

"Wow, that's some storm rolling in," Zara stopped at a window. "Think this is all from that moon?"

"Blood Orange Moon?" Ryan corrected, looking out the same window worriedly. "Yeah. It probably is."

Benny didn't have time to worry about the storm. She switched on the lights as the rain started to patter against the window. All three walls of bookcases lit up, and she, Zara, and Ryan stared at them reverently.

This book is in here, Benny thought, feeling a tingling sensation in her hands. "I never looked for a copy of *Treasure Island*, so why don't we each take a wall and see if we can find it?" she suggested.

"You mean the books aren't in alphabetical order?" Zara asked.

"Are they in *any* kind of order?" Ryan added.

"I'm afraid not," Benny said, climbing one of the moving ladders attached to the shelves. "The book could be anywhere."

Zara put her hands on her hips. "Then I guess we better start searching."

They got to work, the rain and thunder serving as background noise. Each one of them found books that weren't *Treasure Island*, but still seemed of interest. *Moby Dick* (1851) had no markings inside. *Gulliver's Travels* (1726) inspired a lively debate, but there was also nothing of note in its pages. And Mary Shelley's *Frankenstein* (1818) sucked Ryan in, who stopped searching and started reading until Zara snapped at him.

"Any luck?" Benny asked, her arms aching after an hour.

"Nothing. Not even a phony door like in the movies, where you press on a book and the wall opens," Ryan said. To demonstrate, he pressed hard on a book and shoved it, but all that happened was the two books next to it fell off the shelf.

"I was excited to find an early edition of *The Adventures of Huckleberry Finn* by Mark Twain. But that doesn't exactly help us here," Zara was three rungs up on her bookcase ladder, nearing the top. "Some of the books on this shelf are much newer." She pulled a brown book off the shelves. "*The Hidden Staircase*, which is Nancy Drew, was written in 1930 long after Evelyn was gone."

"My grandma gave me some of her old Nancy Drew books to read," Benny said wistfully. *Look around for the clues*, Grams taught her. But what were the clues in this room?

"Maybe the book isn't here," Ryan said.

Please be here she thought. She wasn't ready to give up yet. Benny pushed thoughts of a guest walking off with the book out of her mind and racked her brain for answers. "Alright. Hear me out: What if the book isn't in plain sight? If Evelyn hid something she wanted me to find two hundred years later, she couldn't risk someone finding it, right?"

"Right," Zara agreed,. "So maybe she hid it somewhere she thought you would look. Read the riddle again."

Benny pulled out the letter from Evelyn. "'Treasure, the object of this game, waits on an island with no name. Find one or two of my favorite tomes sitting somewhere in my home. Take care to read behind the lines for that first clue, so bound to find.'"

"'*Sitting* somewhere in my home,'" Ryan repeated. "Let's check the chair cushions!" He lifted both leather chairs, and the cushions didn't budge. "I don't feel anything hard in this seat, but we could slice them open and check the stuffing."

"No!" Benny said. *I can't afford to replace those chairs if he's wrong.* "But maybe there is something to the *sitting* line." She walked over to the window bench and started to feel around.

"I'll keep pressing on books," Ryan said, running at another bookshelf and sending books flying.

"You do that," Zara deadpanned and joined Benny at the window bench. "You might be on to something. Many old homes have built-in, and many, pre-war, had hidden compartments."

A hidden compartment. Benny knocked on the bench. "It sounds hollow."

Zara grinned. "Which means it's the perfect place to hide something." She lifted the top cushion on the bench and frowned. "This is solid on top. We could try to hammer it open though."

"No," Benny said again. She wasn't tearing apart this house if she didn't have to. "Maybe there is another way in." She pulled at a piece of wide-lipped decorative molding on the front of the bench, and it snapped off, revealing a hollow interior. She stuck her hand inside. Immediately she started feeling around.

"Anything?" Zara said, sounding excited as she shined her light onto the small opening.

"There could be rats or bugs in there," Ryan said nervously. "Definitely bugs. We get big water bugs out here."

And just when Benny was ready to say no, her fingers latched on to something soft, like a pillow. "I've got something!" she said, pulling out a sack closed with twine. *This is it. This is it*, Benny thought as she unwrapped the package.

Two books were nestled inside: *Treasure Island* and *Robinson Crusoe*. The brown frayed edges of the leather spines told her the editions were old; the gold lettering had faded, but the titles were clear. Benny's heart started to thud in her chest.

"Yes!" Zara crowed.

"Holy crap," Ryan said, stunned. "Wait, what's the second book?"

"*Robinson Crusoe*?" Benny said, holding it up. "I don't know this one."

"Hang on," said Zara, searching on her phone. "Okay so

get this: *Robinson Crusoe* was first published in 1719, and it's about a castaway who gets trapped on a deserted island for twenty-eight years before being rescued."

A strange sensation prickled at the back of Benny's neck. *Rescued? Why did Evelyn pick that book? Is there a reason?*

Ryan took the book from Benny and shook the pages. "No letter or note though. You'd think she'd leave one if this was a clue."

He was right. Benny dusted the book off and felt her heart start to pump wildly as she cracked open the spine on *Treasure Island*, waiting for a letter or diary pages to fall out. Instead, she found nothing there either. "'Read behind the lines,'" Benny repeated. "That was in the clue too."

We're missing something, Benny thought, flipping through *Treasure Island* page by page. "Evelyn went through a lot of trouble to hide two books about pirates and deserted islands in this window bench in a room that was original to her house. There has to be a message in here, somewhere." Lightning flashed, and that's when she noticed a short sentence on the inside binding in the back of *Treasure Island*. "Wait! Look!"

Ryan opened the other book again. The same wording appeared in that book as well. "It's in *Crusoe* too!" Ryan said, excited.

Zara read the tiny marking. "'High tide three low tide.' What does that mean?"

"It's the time till low tide," Ryan explained. "It means there are three hours till the next low tide." She and Zara looked at him. "I know how to read a tide clock. My dad is a boater. He lives by one of these."

"Greenport is a big fishing village—or was one once," Zara mused. "This could mean something. But why no letter? How do you find the clue without one?"

"Maybe the books aren't the actual clue. Just a way to find it." Benny stood up, feeling like she was closer. She needed to break down what she knew. The books were about treasure and castaways, in the library that had been there since the house was built, hidden away for her to find a written message. *It's a clue meant to lead me to the actual prize, isn't it?* She looked around at the room again, thinking of everything old and new, and her eyes landed on the strange clock on the mantel. She lunged for it and held it up. "Isn't this a tide clock? It was Evelyn's."

"Yes! Let's move the dials to the numbers in the book." Ryan took the clock from her. "Maybe if you move it to the exact time as the book..."

Her heart was beating faster now, like the rain that sounded like a stampede. She watched Ryan turn the dials, the little image of a seaport moving with the changing of the time, and then Ryan clicked the numbers into position and pressed in the dial.

As he did, the bottom of the clock popped open. Out fell an envelope.

For Everly Benedict.
Enclosed is your second riddle.

Benny swooped down to pick it up, her fingers trembling as she saw the familiar handwriting and the inscription on the thick aged envelope. Carefully she opened it and realized something else was inside: a key.

"What do you think that's for?" Zara whispered, staring at the small gold key with interest.

Benny was equally intrigued. Her stomach felt like a ship at sea, swooping back and forth. "I don't know but I'm hoping this letter tells us."

"Hurry up and read it!" Ryan said excitedly. "And read it aloud."

His excitement was contagious. Benny cleared her throat. "Here it goes. Everly..."

June 17, 1850

Everly,

Congratulations! You've passed my first test.

I knew you could do it. And if you've played the game this far, hopefully you're willing to go further.

Hidden in this tide clock are more entries from my journal. My hope is they will help you understand what happened in those days after I met Kimble and learned about his curse. I say *curse* because while you may read my story and think, *Pirate! Treasure! Adventure afoot!* as if we were part of *Robinson Crusoe* (a book that delighted me in my youth), this treasure I speak of comes at a high cost.

I'm hopeful that by sharing my journal, you will understand why I made the choices I did. There are those who call me selfish for what happened, but even now I choose to think I was brave. Sacrificing everything you love to save what's most important is not easy. I will live with the choices I made for the rest of my life and pray that by the time you come along, together we will have found a way to right my wrongs.

But if you ask me even now, in my thirties, a mother myself, if I wished Captain Kimble and my island had never appeared at all, I would tell you no. As my friend Aggy once said, some things are meant to be.

I will say nothing more in case this letter falls into the wrong hands, but be careful who you trust, and be mindful of the ticking clock. Time waits for no one, I'm afraid. And as I've learned, sometimes the journey is more important than the final destination.

This riddle comes with a tool to aid you: this key.

So godspeed, Everly Benedict, and may luck help you with your second riddle.

Somewhere in this house is a door hidden from view.

Though it has no locks, you'll need the key to get through.

> With much respect and
>
> admiration,
>
> Evelyn Terry

TWELVE

BENNY

PRESENT DAY

Benny read Evelyn's latest letter at least twenty times. She turned the small key over and over in her hands wondering what it would lead to. She picked apart each sentence in the letter, laboring over each word, trying to decode the message Evelyn left her.

Her. Everly Benedict.

If she'd needed proof before that this game was truly meant to be played by her, now she was certain. Her great-great-great-great-great-grandmother had written letters to her personally one hundred and seventy-five years before she was born.

But even though the new riddle was shorter, it was even

more confusing than the last one. A door with no locks that needed a key to get through? What did that mean?

The three of them searched the entire downstairs of the house with military precision, looking for a door with no locks that needed a key, but there were no doors that fit that description. Then they checked the doors on the second floor, but still nothing. It was getting close to dinner, and both Zara and Ryan had to get home.

"We'll come back tomorrow," Zara promised. "I can be here by noon. I promised my grandmother I'd help her sort through some donations to the museum that came this week in the morning."

"Noon is great." Benny looked at the journal pages in her hands again, shuffling from one entry to the other. Something was gnawing at her and she wasn't sure if she should mention it.

"You're making that face again," Zara said.

"What face?" Benny asked.

Zara grinned. "That one where you're deciding if you should say something out loud or keep it to yourself."

Wow, she knows me already, Benny thought.

"I didn't notice you make a face," Ryan said gently.

"Is it something in the journal?" Zara prodded. "Did you find something?"

"It's Evelyn's journal entries," Benny explained. "They're numbered incorrectly. These are two and four. Where is three?"

"Let me see," said Ryan. Zara came over to look as well. They shuffled through the pages, gentle with the aging paper. "They're misnumbered alright. Probably just an accident."

"Is it?" Zara said, and Benny could almost see the wheels in her brain turning. "What if she did it on purpose?"

"I guess read the pages and then you'll know for sure," Ryan suggested.

"True," Benny said, pushing a stray piece of her brown hair behind her ear, like her mom did when she was anxious. Benny was definitely anxious. "I'll let you know what I find." Tomorrow she would only have seven days left to complete the game.

Benny tried to stay calm and remember that for the first time ever, she was part of a team. She wasn't alone in this quest. She had friends her own age to help her and that felt...nice. If unfamiliar. Maybe unfamiliar was good, in case she lost and didn't get to stay in Greenport, in this beautiful house, near new friends. She felt the panic rising again. What if the island wasn't real?

It is real, she told herself.

Once everyone left, Benny sat down to read Evelyn's new journal entries. She read them twice then she decided Zara was right—Evelyn must have mismarked them. The second entry introduced her to Evelyn's Papa and Axel Rudd, while the third took place the next morning, when Evelyn went to the island to meet Kimble and ask him questions. She was pretty sure there wasn't an entry missing in-between.

The entries themselves made Benny surer than ever—Kimble, as impossible as it sounded, had stayed the same age for two hundred years. Which made Benny wonder—had he found whatever he was looking for and lived out his life already? Was he long dead and buried now too? Or was he still alive? And if so, where was he?

Benny heard her phone buzz, and she picked it up when she saw it was one of the (now) five numbers she had stored in her phone. "Hi, Peter."

"Benny! Just thought I'd check in and see how everything was going." She pictured him in a ball cap and jeans, with his feet up (sneakers for sure) on a desk, leaning back in his chair like a kid. "Your mom told me you are enjoying Summerville and all the estate has to offer."

Benny's mom walked by just then, humming to herself and wearing tennis whites, of all things. "Yes, some of us more than others," Benny said.

"Good! How is the game going? Are you making progress?"

"I found the first clue yesterday, and it came with another riddle, more journal pages, and a second letter addressed to me," she said, watching her mom go straight to the kitchen cabinet with the water bottles. She pulled one out to take to… tennis? Did her mom play tennis now?

"Really? That's great! Wait till I tell the office." Peter sounded as excited as she was yesterday. "You're making progress, and you've still got a week."

One week. One week. One week. The words screamed in her head. She took a deep breath. "Yes, I know I can find the island in time," Benny said firmly.

"I know you will. But Benny? If you need anything, please don't hesitate to call. I'll check in again in a few days."

Hanging up, Benny unfolded her legs from under her and made her way to her mom. She looked like one of the guests at the inn. "Tennis?" Benny asked.

"No." Her mom smiled, her blue eyes crinkling. "Believe it or not, Harris is teaching me pickleball."

"No! Not you too!" Benny laughed. Wally said every new guest who came to the inn asked if there was a pickleball court.

"It's fun! You should try it," Mom said. "Actually, Harris and I were saying maybe the four of us could play—you and me versus him and Ryan?"

Benny's insides did an unwelcome flutter. *Your mother has a new boyfriend*, Grams used to say. *We'll see her again when this one bites the dust.* Her mother loved falling in love. It was staying in love that seemed to be the problem. She'd never met her father. And Benny was happy the boyfriends she remembered didn't stick around. None were worthy of her mom. But Harris seemed different. He was an accomplished businessman. Her mom deserved someone nice showing her around Greenport. *And if I win the game, she can stay here. We both can.* "Pickleball would be fun," Benny said. She wasn't sure Ryan would agree. "*Mom*," she said excitedly, since she hadn't seen her since yesterday, "we found the second clue."

"You did? Why didn't you tell me?" her mom said, sounding animated, her ponytail swaying. "Wait. Tell me while we play a quick game." She went over to the counter and brought over a stacking game. Their version happened to be wood blocks that looked like skeleton bones (Grams bought it. She was quirky that way.) "An oldie but a goodie."

Her mom stacked the tower of slim bone-shaped blocks and removed the first piece from the middle of the tower and placed it on top. Benny went next. Each move made the tower less stable, but Benny was strategic, looking for pieces that were looser and easier to move. The first person to knock it over lost the game. They hadn't played this one in a while. Benny filled her mom in on the library, *Treasure Island*, *Robinson Crusoe*, and the tide clock as they played, along with what she'd read in the new journal pages. The block tower stacked higher and higher.

"So are you saying Evelyn thinks this Kimble is immortal? And that the island might be supernatural since only she seems able to find it?" Her mom stuck a piece precariously on the top of the tower.

Hearing her mother say it out loud made Benny realize how bonkers it all sounded. "It looks that way, but I only have a few of her journal entries, so I'm not sure. I think Evelyn is trying to tell me her story and about who Kimble is in pieces, revealing more with each riddle. She seems afraid of the journal falling in the wrong hands.

"How do the pages you have end?" Mom asked, a wrinkle appearing above her brow as she tried hard to understand.

"The last page I have ended with Kimble and Evelyn's conversation about the island being interrupted by her friend Aggy." Benny carefully pried out a bone near the bottom of the tower and placed it on top.

Mom took a sip of coffee and then made her next move. "And you're sure the journal pages aren't fiction? Maybe she was writing a novel."

"I don't think so. Why would she want me to read the pages or say they're from her journal if they aren't part of her story? No, I think Evelyn wants me to understand why it's so important I find her island. Something is on it she must want me to find. I just don't know what yet." Benny drummed her fingers on the countertop and looked out the kitchen window at the inn guests enjoying a rare morning of no rain. At that moment, her mom placed a new bone on top, and the tower came tumbling down.

"I win!" Benny crowed just as the doorbell rang, loud and long, like a gong.

"I'll get it," Wally said pleasantly, moving to the door and opening it as she and Mom picked up the pieces. "Hello, Harris, Ryan. Ladies, you have company."

"Hello! I hope we're not interrupting," Harris said, walking into the kitchen. "What are you two doing? Playing a game?"

"We love games," Mom told him. "It's our thing."

Harris smiled. "It's certainly Benny's, as Evelyn Terry seemed to predict." He stared at her a beat. "Sorry to interrupt, but we have a ten-thirty pickleball lesson, so I brought Ryan early so he wouldn't have to bike. It's supposed to rain later. I hope that's okay."

"Of course. Right, Benny?" Mom said, looking at her pleadingly.

"Of course." Benny wasn't used to having people over. There was no room in their rentals, and she hadn't had a play-date since she was little and they lived with Grams. What were they supposed to do while they waited for Zara to arrive?

"Any cookies?" Ryan asked, looking around. He was wearing another Hawaiian shirt and had on cutoff shorts and flip-flops. "Those were really good yesterday."

"*Ryan*," Harris admonished.

"What?" Ryan looked embarrassed. "Wally's cookies were awesome."

At this, Wally chuckled. "I'm happy to make more for today's clue hunting."

Harris turned to Benny. "Yes, Ryan said you made progress. Though his lips were sealed about what you found."

"Benny said to keep it between us." Ryan looked at her and smiled as Wally gave him a glass of milk. "I don't want to get kicked off the team."

Team. This was the first time she'd ever been on one. She felt a thrill at the thought. But then she remembered Evelyn's warning in the second letter: *Be careful who you trust.* Why? Who could she have been worried about?

"We should get going." Mom kissed her on the cheek. "Good luck today, you two. Let me know what you find."

"I'm going to get some cookie dough out of the inn freezer and bake you three a new batch," Wally said, leaving her in the kitchen with Ryan, who started gulping down milk like it was water.

"So what should we do while we wait for Zara?" Ryan asked. "Sorry I'm early. My dad insisted on driving me." He rolled his eyes.

"It's alright," Benny told him. "I guess we can walk the grounds. Maybe play a game? I don't really want to start searching till Zara gets here."

Ryan nodded. "What kind of game? The block thing?" He pointed to the skeleton game on the table. "That's cool. Like Jenga. We can play *and* try to crack Evelyn's riddle."

Benny dumped the contents out on the counter. "I like that idea," she said, stacking pieces again. She had the tower up in no time.

"Did you read Evelyn's new journal entries?" Ryan asked as he placed a bone on the top of the tower.

"Several times," Benny admitted as she slid another block from its place. "It was more about Kimble and the island, but nothing that tells me why she wants me to find this place so badly. I hope there are more entries when we find the next clue."

"What about the misnumbered entries?" Ryan asked. "Does it look like something is missing?"

Benny shook her head. "I don't think so. One entry is June fourth and the next is June fifth. I think it was just a mistake."

"Want me to take a look to be sure?" Ryan asked, concentrating on a block that was stuck in place.

Benny hesitated. Yes, Zara had read the letter and Ryan had read the second one when they'd found the first clue. But there was something about Evelyn's journal entries that still felt so private. She wasn't ready to share them with anyone and she wasn't sure why. "Thanks. It's okay."

He looked at her searchingly.

Be careful who you trust. "Evelyn was so secretive. I know it sounds silly, but I feel like I'm betraying her somehow by showing you her private journals. Does that make sense?"

"I get it," Ryan said, knocking the tower over on his next turn. He groaned. "You win."

"Rematch?" Ryan nodded and Benny started to restack the blocks. "While I'm setting the game up, maybe you can tell me what you think of this key that was with the letter." That was something she didn't mind showing him. She'd been staring at it all morning herself and had no clue what it could be for. She pulled it out of her pocket.

There was heft to it, and for some reason, Benny felt the key was important not just for the riddle but in understanding

Evelyn. It was small, a burnished gold with a decorative piece at the top that looked like a small fleur-de-lis. The key itself was thin, but the metal was heavy, and the bottom piece, the locking mechanism, was shaped like a small C.

Ryan flipped it over in his hands. "Seems too small for a door lock. Maybe a safe? Or a cabinet? Did you check the bookcases in the library again?"

"We did that yesterday," Benny reminded him, taking the key and placing it back in her pocket.

"Evelyn mentioned treasure in the first clue." Ryan made the first move on the new game. "Maybe the key is to a treasure chest?"

"On the island?" Benny wondered for a second. "I guess it could be, but she said we needed the key for the next clue, so it has to be something with can find. There's no sign of the island yet."

"Wouldn't it be cool if there was a treasure chest?" Ryan said wistfully. "Then you'd be mega rich. The house, the grounds, the money, *and* buried treasure. If it's Kimble's, it would be worth a fortune."

"Maybe," Benny said. "But I'm not really in the game for the money."

Ryan looked surprised. "You're not?"

"I mean, yes, we need money," Benny clarified.

Benny looked around at the kitchen with its state-of-the-art appliances, new cabinets, and open floor plan to a family room, a dining area, a den, and a pool outside the windows. A few acres away was the inn she'd own, the vineyard, and so much more. But it wasn't any of that she was really interested in keeping. "I don't need a fortune. Just enough to live here. What I want," she said slowly, "is to finally have a home my mom and I can call our own. I know it sounds silly." She felt her cheeks flush. "But having a house of our own is something I've always dreamed about. And a life in Greenport looks like a place we both would feel at home."

Ryan studied her for a moment. "It doesn't sound silly at all." He put down the blocks in his hands. "Let's make sure you win so that happens."

GREENPORT HERALD

June 15, 1825

MISSING: AXEL RUDD

BY HENRY STEVENS

Shipping magnate Elias Rudd is in need of the community's help. His fourteen-year-old son, Axel Rudd, went missing the night of the Blood Orange Moon. He has brown hair, brown eyes, pale skin, and was last seen wearing a white button-down shirt with suspenders and brown pants from the Greenport Mercantile. On the night in question, he left his father a note saying he was seeing his friend Evelyn Terry. The Terry family insists their daughter was at home, as many families in Greenport have kept their children at home to avoid catching the Cough. The Rudd family is offering a reward for their son's safe return.

THIRTEEN

BENNY

PRESENT DAY

Zara arrived at Summerville in the middle of a sudden down-pour. "My grandma dropped me off," she told Benny. "She didn't want me getting caught in the storm on my bike." She shook out her long curly brown hair as a rumble seemed to rock the house.

Wally took her wet jacket and umbrella and offered her a warm cookie.

"Thanks," she said and looked at Benny. "I like him."

"Me too," said Benny with a smile, and Wally winked at her.

"Eat your cookie and let's go." Ryan bounced up and down on his toes. He was clearly hopped up on sugar. "We have a riddle to solve."

"Slow your roll. I have some news that might help." Zara reached into her black backpack, covered in pins and patches, and pulled out a small stack of paper. "My grandma printed out these news articles from the *Greenport Herald* that were in the archives." She looked at me. "Get this: looks like Elias Rudd, who owned the fish factory and the docks in the 1800s, blamed Evelyn for his son's disappearance. Axel Rudd was never seen again after the Blood Orange Moon."

Ryan stopped hopping. "He died because of the moon?"

"No, but the weather could have had something to do with it. Maybe he drowned." Zara looked at Benny. "According to the archives, Axel Rudd went missing and was never found. Weirdly, he wasn't the only kid to go missing around that time, but there's not much known about the others."

Benny glanced at the article. "Why would they only report Axel if there were others?"

Zara shrugged. "Maybe it's because they weren't from the richest family in town. Elias Rudd, however, pretty much ran Greenport and he was convinced Evelyn had something to do with his son's disappearance."

Benny held the printed page tighter. Evelyn knew Axel. Her new journal entry mentioned him calling on her. She also wrote about how he couldn't find the island on his own and how she couldn't stand him. Did she have something to do with his disappearance? "Did Evelyn ever publicly say if she knew what happened to Axel?" Benny asked calmly.

"Not that we could find," Zara said, tapping the paper in Benny's hands. "Her parents swore she was home the night Axel disappeared. He could have run off. Grams said kids did that back then, running off to the city. There was also an outbreak of whooping cough, which they called "the Cough" around that time. There were so many deaths between that and the Blood Orange Moon that not every person was accounted for."

"But Elias was still convinced Evelyn knew something. Why?" Ryan wondered.

"That is where the story gets interesting." Zara handed Benny more papers. "My grandma said she's heard rumors for years about Evelyn and Axel searching for buried treasure together." Her eyes flashed. "And not just any buried treasure; treasure that could make you immortal."

"Like the Fountain of Youth?" Ryan asked, his eyes wide as rain began to pound the roof.

Zara grinned. "Bingo." She looked at Benny. This is wild! For centuries people have gone in search of the Fountain of Youth, but I've never heard of it being tied to Long Island. I left a message for my parents though, asking if they ever heard anything about treasure rumored to be the

Fountain of Youth. I don't know if we'll hear back from them though. Where they are in the British Virgin Islands has real spotty Wi-Fi."

Benny glanced at the headline for the missing Axel Rudd. There was also an article about a Cough outbreak in Greenport. Obviously, nothing about a Fountain of Youth. But... could the rumors Zara's grandma heard be true? Is that why Evelyn wanted her to find the island?

"Does Evelyn mention any of this in her journal?" Ryan asked.

"Nothing about a Fountain of Youth," Benny said, being truthful. She felt a twinge of guilt again for not sharing the entries with them. Zara hadn't asked, but Ryan had. The journals felt too personal to share yet.

"Her letter just talks about how important it is that I find the island by the deadline," Zara said, thinking aloud. "She also mentions a curse, but I don't know what she means by that. Do you?"

Benny shook her head. Evelyn had used the word "curse" before, but Benny still didn't know what it meant. Suddenly she felt more confused than ever. Maybe it would help if she shared the pages. *Evelyn said to be careful who you trust*, she reminded herself. "The last journal page I read talks about Aggy, Evelyn's best friend, coming to find her when she snuck off to talk to Kimble."

"Aggy…" Zara thought for a moment. "What's her last name?"

"Evelyn doesn't give one, which is odd, because everyone else she writes about has a last name," Benny said, realizing this aloud. That was odd, wasn't it?

"Aggy No Last Name. This story gets more and more interesting by the moment," Zara said as the lights in the house flickered from the storm. "Evelyn is tricky to figure out."

"So are her riddles," Ryan said. "And Benny won't get more journal pages to read till we solve the next riddle."

Benny shifted from one foot to the other, feeling uncomfortable. Why was she keeping the journal pages to herself? Was it Evelyn's warning? Or something else bothering her? *What's wrong with me?* she wondered. Here she was, keeping the journal pages from them, and all Zara and Ryan wanted to do was help her. The lights flickered again.

"Don't worry! We have a pretty good generator!" Wally called from the other room.

Evelyn, Benny thought, *what are you not telling me?* She glanced at a painting of a black bird on the entrance hall wall and wondered who this "Sparrow" really was. She didn't want to think the worst of her ancestor, but this new information about Axel Rudd going missing when he was with Evelyn made her a little uneasy. Evelyn was keeping secrets, and Benny was determined to find out what they were. "Ryan's right. If we want answers, we need to solve this riddle." Benny pulled the key out of her pocket. "Something in this house must fit this key."

Wally walked over with a tray of cups and a pitcher of iced tea, and stared at the key. "That looks mighty old."

"It was Evelyn's," Benny explained. "Any ideas on where to look? We've tried all the locks we can find here. Maybe this comes from the inn?"

Wally shook his head. "The inn was built much later. The oldest building is this house." He peered closer at it. "Did you try the attic?"

Benny did a double take. "The house has an attic?"

The lights flickered some more, and the rain sounded like someone had dropped a bucket of nails on the roof.

"Wow, it's getting bad out there," Ryan said nervously.

Wally put down the tray and started walking toward the stairs. "Part of the rules of the house: Evelyn's trust says the attic's contents can't be removed."

"So things belonging to Evelyn are still up there?" Benny asked, excitement mounting as she rushed after him with Zara and Ryan right behind her. She grabbed her camera from a table by the stairs. "Are there doors up there? Or doors with no locks that need a key?" Her heart was thumping now. She was getting closer.

Wally chuckled. "Why don't you check? The space isn't finished, so I've had no need to go up there myself." He reached the second-floor landing, then headed down the hall, while Benny and her friends followed.

Thunder cracked, and Ryan banged into Benny as the lights went out for a second, then came on again. It was darker on the second floor than it was downstairs.

"Maybe we shouldn't go up to the attic until after the storm passes?" Ryan suggested. "In case the lights go out."

"Are you kidding? When there is an attic to explore that possibly has all the answers?" Zara said, looking a bit like her grandmother in that moment.

"Yeah, we can't wait when we're running out of time," Benny said as the lights flickered again and the ground beneath them seemed to rumble like a freight train.

Wally made it to the end of the hall and opened a large closet, then turned on the light. Benny held her breath, hoping to see an attic door needing a key. Instead, she saw a small square opening above their heads with a pull string. No key required. Wally yanked on it, and very narrow metal stairs unfolded like an accordion. The lights went out again and back on.

"But maybe we should turn on our phone flashlights," Benny suggested.

"And take the cookies," Ryan said, and she turned to see he'd brought the plate with him.

Wally held the stairs steady. "Be careful. I don't want to tell your parents that someone got hurt up there."

Benny went first. Zara was right behind her. "Wish us luck, Wally."

"What if there are spiders up there? There has to be spiders, don't you think?" Ryan asked, joining the climb. Benny could hear the wind howling now.

"There's definitely going to be spiders," Zara said with glee. "I'll protect you."

Just then the thunder boomed so loud, it sounded like the storm was directly over the house now. Ryan whimpered.

"Ryan, don't be a baby. It's just a storm." Zara pressed the flashlight button on her phone and shined it upward as she reached the top step. Benny helped her up. "This isn't...creepy at all." Zara's voice sounded funny now too.

Benny turned on the flashlight button on her phone and held it out to see the attic. The narrow room had low eaves and a chimney at one end of the room. Two small windows at each end of the attic barely provided any light. With their flashlights, Benny could make out several trunks, furniture covered by sheets, and paintings. A mixture of heat and musty old-stuff smell was converging in the space. The sound of rain was louder too.

"Yes! There's a light switch," said Ryan, pulling the chain on the single bulb in the center of the room. The light flickered on and off and popped, plummeting the room back into darkness.

ENTRY 5

From Evelyn Terry's Private Journal,
Dated June 6, 1825

> Aggy knew what I'd done. And for
> reasons I didn't yet understand, she
> was keeping secrets from me too...

"Sparrow!" I could hear Aggy shouting for me as I left the fort on the island.

I ran, thundering down the rocky path with Winks in my arms. I was trying to put as much distance between myself and Kimble and this mysterious fort that had appeared out of nowhere before Aggy spotted us. Rounding the bend at the bottom of the hill, I found Aggy waiting for me. She didn't look like her usual self, but I didn't yet understand why.

"You went to see him," she said accusingly, and we both knew who she was talking about without saying his name.

Winks jumped from my arms with a loud meow and slinked over to my friend. Aggy didn't seem pleased with her either. "Traitor," she said to the cat. "I know you went to see him too." Winks hissed at her.

"You told me not to tell the others what I saw," I argued. "You didn't say *I* couldn't return to the island to talk to him."

Aggy gave a deep sigh. "*Sparrow*," she said wearily as if to say, *What am I going to do with you?* She looked tired, as if she hadn't slept the night before either. She was wearing her white dress, the one she always washed for school, and her beautiful brown curls blew in the warm breeze. The sunny sky on our island masked the truth of the weather in Greenport—more rain, more storms. She and I, it seemed, were the only two people who could find their way to the island on their own and enjoy its spoils. I looked up at the sun, basking in its glow. "You shouldn't be here. We have school," she reminded me, picking up Winks, who tried to claw her way out of her arms. She sounded like my mama.

"I'm not late. Class hasn't started yet," I said stubbornly and bit my lower lip, hesitating. What I was about to say would sound absurd, but so did seeing a pirate ship no one else could see. "Aggy...the man told me his name. It's Jonas Kimble." She was quiet. "He says he's *the* Jonas Kimble. The famous pirate from the 1600s, but he looks Papa's age. Younger! That's impossible, isn't it?"

Aggy stared at her bare feet and said nothing.

"Tell me it's impossible," I pressed, growing anxious as Winks calmed and watched me from Aggy's arms. "Tell me, Aggy."

"I can't," she blurted. "Because he *is* Captain Kimble. I have seen him in my dreams." Aggy closed her eyes as if in pain. "Several times, in fact. Mama has too. He and the island, they are tied together."

"What does that mean?" I asked as I tried to ignore the island whispering my name again.

Her face twisted as if she was fighting to find the words. "This island was his long before it was ours. And it belonged to someone before him too. And now..." She trailed off. "I didn't mention knowing who he was yesterday because I wanted to deny it. Just like I tried to ignore my dreams. But Mama explained...this is meant to be. It is what has to happen if we're to have a future." She looked at me again, and I saw there were tears in her eyes. Winks meowed mournfully as if she understood what Aggy was saying. "This is the only way to save us."

"Save us?" I didn't understand.

"Gil. Thomas. Laurel." Aggy seemed sad. "You are going to be fine. Kimble will be too...eventually. He still has more he needs to do first." Her eyes were pleading. "Please don't fight this. You need to let fate take its course."

"What do you mean?" I snapped. She was frightening me.

Aggy unhooked the locket around her neck. It had an *A* inscribed on the front. "I want you to have this."

"Your locket? No. That's yours," I protested. The chain was her one luxury, a simple silver chain and locket her father had given her when she moved to Greenport, before he died. I knew it meant the world to her.

"I want you to hold on to it," she insisted and started to cough. "It will come back to me someday."

I paled. Was Aggy sick? "You're scaring me."

"Don't be scared. Be brave. You're the bravest of all of us, Sparrow. Your job is going to be the hardest, but I know you were made to do hard things. I've explained what's going to happen in this letter," Aggy told me. "Keep it safe! Share it with no one. I only wrote it because Mama said you would want to hear everything from me before..." Her face scrunched up, and I thought she might cry. "Please read this after I'm gone." She held the letter out to me.

I wouldn't touch it. "Gone? Where are you going? Are you leaving Greenport?"

She shook her head. "Not exactly. But after the Blood Orange Moon, you won't see me again."

"Why not? What is going to happen on the Blood Orange Moon?" I demanded.

Aggy shook her head harder and tried not to cry. "Please. I don't want to speak of it. Just take the locket, and read my letter after. It will bring you peace."

"Are you dying?" I said, starting to cry now.

"No!" Aggy insisted, and Winks meowed louder. "Not dying. We just won't... Look, I can't explain. It's all in this letter. Take it. Please."

"No! I am tired of your riddles!" I backed away, frightened by the truth I knew Aggy's sight foretold in that letter. "I don't want to hear anything about you leaving! Or our friends! Maybe your sight is wrong. Maybe the man in the fort is lying about treasure!"

Aggy's eyes widened. "He told you about the treasure? And you found the fort on your own? I didn't see that happening in my vision."

"You know about these things?" I felt betrayed. "Why didn't you tell me who he was yesterday?"

"Sparrow, I—" Aggy started to say, but I didn't want to hear any more.

I was so angry. I turned and ran away from my best

friend on one of the last days we'd be together. Off the island I rushed across the sandbar, the warm sun disappearing behind dark clouds as I returned to the real world. A light mist fell in Greenport, heavy fog draping everything in mystery. I could hear Aggy calling for me again, but I didn't care. I just kept running till I finally reached the path between both our roads home. That's where I cried in earnest.

I may not have had the gift of sight like Aggy, but even I could tell that between the island, Kimble, and the Blood Orange Moon's imminent arrival, things were changing. And I didn't want them to. For some reason, even then, I knew I was the one about to be left behind. I heard a meow and looked down. Winks was winding her way around my legs, the orange tabby meowing urgently. She reached out a claw and swiped my leg, drawing blood.

"What is wrong with you, cat?" I barked, and the cat took off, back toward the island.

I watched her hurry over to something on the ground, and I paled.

"Aggy!" I cried. When I reached her side, she was coughing violently. She held a linen handkerchief to her mouth, and when she removed it, I saw it was covered with blood.

"Stay where you are!" she told me. Winks sat down beside

her, watching me like a hawk. "No closer. You can't get sick, Sparrow."

I sunk down on the sand nearby. "Neither can you," I said, frightened. Why hadn't I noticed how pale she looked? "I'm sorry I yelled. I'm so sorry, Aggy. I won't leave you here."

"It's alright, Sparrow. I'm not alone. Winks will wait with me. Go get my mama," she said, lying back on the sand and closing her eyes.

"Alright," I promised, standing up again and running, tears streaming down my cheeks as I thought of Aggy succumbing to the Cough.

I knew then I would do everything in my power to prevent that from happening.

The Cough was coming for all of us, and I was determined to stop it.

FOURTEEN

BENNY

PRESENT DAY

"Did you see that?" Ryan was freaking out. "We got up to the attic and *BOOM*! The lights go out. Creepy. Definitely creepy!"

"Or it was it just an old light bulb?" Zara guessed, but even Benny had to admit her heart was beating faster now.

"Power is out," Wally called up to her. "I'll see what's taking the generator so long."

"Great," Ryan mumbled. "This sounds like the start to every horror movie." He started to fan himself. "Is it hot up here? It *feels* hot up here. And sometimes when it's hot or I get really anxious, I pass out."

"Yeah, I remember that from science class," Zara noted.

"That day we were dissecting fetal pigs, I literally lifted my scalpel and *boom*! You were out like a light."

"Because it was hot," Ryan said hurriedly. "Not because I was nervous about... Ugh. I can't think about that day. The smell of formaldehyde alone..."

"Just focus on the riddle," Benny told him, her voice soothing. "A door with no locks that needs a key to get through."

"Even though it doesn't make sense," Zara reminded her.

"Good riddles are never easy," Benny said, shining her light over several portraits. She picked up one to examine. It was a painting of a boy on a beach with sandy blond hair and a bright smile. In his hand was a small purple cloth pouch. The style of the painting was similar to the self-portrait Evelyn had done of herself that hung in the library. She saw the insignia on the bottom right: *EVELYN TERRY 1850. That's the same year the trust was made* Benny realized She flipped it over to see if the painting had a fake back or any openings. That could be where the next answer was waiting. Nothing was there.

"Who is that?" Zara asked, shining a light on the canvas.

"I'm not sure, but it's another one of Evelyn's. She painted it the same year she set up the inheritance. I think she painted all of these." There was another painting of two people behind the first one. These individuals were also on a beach. They looked older—a teen boy with brown hair wearing suspenders and a collared shirt, and a girl with long black hair, her arms wrapped around his waist. They were holding purple cloth bags too. The girl was looking up at the boy and smiling. It was also dated 1850.

"It feels like a series of paintings all with different people in the same spot on a beach. Maybe the island?" Zara crouched down and moved the painting aside to reveal another painting. This boy, with dark eyes and jet-black hair, had a serious expression. The sky above him was stormy like his eyes, which seemed angry. Unlike the others, he did not have a small bag in his hand.

"I think this is Axel Rudd," Zara said. "There's a drawing of him in one of the articles I gave you, and this is very similar."

Benny's felt her shoulders tighten. "It does look like him. That's odd, right?"

"Odd to paint a picture of someone whose dad thinks you made him disappear?" Zara asked. "Yes."

"Maybe she felt guilty," Ryan suggested.

"Or she didn't do it, and this proves he was her friend," Zara argued.

Benny wasn't sure either of them were right. Evelyn's journal mentioned her not being fond of Axel. Why would she paint a portrait of him? *We're missing something. What are you trying to tell me, Evelyn?* "Still not what we're looking for though," Benny reminded them and left the painting behind to sort through a box of mirrors and other trinkets. "Let's spread out and search."

They turned in different directions and began examining boxes. Their phone lights bounced off the walls as did the lightning, making Benny feel like they were at a light show. She was afraid to miss something, so she looked through every box of clothing, at every old toy and hat. They worked quietly for a bit, listening to the sound of rain hitting the roof. Thunder cracked loud overhead, and Ryan shrieked. The next sound Benny heard was breaking glass.

"Sorry! Sorry! Sorry!" Ryan said as they all rushed over to see what he'd broken.

"RYAN!" Zara moaned again. "If you break something, Evelyn is going to haunt you!"

"Seriously?" Ryan asked, eyes wide. "You are kidding, right? Okay, I'm starting to feel woozy. The heat up here is getting to me."

"There are no ghosts, Ryan." Benny flashed her light on a coatrack, which held top hats and assorted ladies' headpieces. "Just a lot of memories up here." She leaned down and picked up the frame Ryan had knocked over. "Thankfully, you only broke a picture frame."

"Which has a map of Long Island in it," Zara pointed out.

Benny felt her fingers tingle. It was a map dated 1825. Was this Evelyn's too? It had frayed edges, and one corner was burned. Even the ink on the map had started to fade. On the top right side of the map was a compass star, and there were small images of boats in the water. Benny spotted something peculiar.

"Look!" she said suddenly. In the center of the two forks was Shelter Island and a small island named Gardiner's Island, but then there was another body of land right off of Greenport, and it had been labeled with an *X* and handwritten words: *EVELYN'S ISLAND.* "Here's where she thinks the island is." The island was tiny compared to Shelter Island and so close to the shore, it looked like one could swim to it. She lifted her camera from around her neck and took a picture of the map.

"There's the island," Zara marveled. "At least where Evelyn thinks it should be."

"Maybe the key she left you is a metaphor for a map key?" Ryan was wearing one of the top hats from the coatrack. "I mean it's a map with Evelyn's island on it, so technically that's a key, right?"

"I see your point, but I don't think so. The key has to fit a lock." She checked the back of the map, but it was clear. "No. If this is where the answer to the riddle is hiding, there has to be something up here we're still missing."

THUD.

Something hard, like a tree branch, had fallen on the roof.

Ryan stumbled backward, the hat tumbling off him as he crashed into a piece of furniture behind him. He reached out to stop himself from falling and wound up grabbing the sheet over the furniture instead. He yanked it clear before he fell.

"Ryan! Again? Seriously!" Zara moaned.

"Wait! This could be good! Look at that dollhouse," Benny said, feeling a prickling sensation in the back of her neck. "It is a miniature version of this house!" Her heart started to beat fast as she rushed over to examine it. "And it has a front door that has no lock, but..."

Zara gasped and dropped down beside her, examining the small doorknob on the door. "The knob has a picture of a key on it."

FIFTEEN

BENNY

The three of them stared at the dollhouse. Was this the answer to the riddle they were looking for?

Something told Benny yes.

The dollhouse was exactly like Evelyn's house, down to the balcony Benny had stood on numerous times, staring out at the water. The piece was well constructed and in good condition. It didn't look like a child's toy. It was more like a showpiece. Inside the windows, Benny could see tiny pieces of furniture.

"I found something good, right?" Ryan asked, standing up and marveling at the toy while he brushed off some of the thick dust, sneezing in the process.

"Maybe." Zara searched the sides of the dollhouse. "We need to find a place to insert the key."

Benny ran her fingers over the small shingles and shutters, her fingers looking for a seam to open the dollhouse and see what was inside. "There are several doors on this but no locks, and yet..." She shined a light on the decorative wreath on the dollhouse's chimney. There was a slim letter-sized opening in the middle of it. "This feels like somewhere you'd place a key." She pulled Evelyn's key out of her pocket and then held her breath as she stuck the end in the wreath.

The wreath turned counterclockwise, and Benny heard a click. The front of the house swung open, revealing the rooms inside. She gave a loud whoop.

"I don't believe it," Zara whispered, eyes wide. "We found it. We actually found the answer to the riddle...and it's a dollhouse."

"No. Way," Ryan whispered.

This was Evelyn's house down to the smallest detail. The furniture was different, but the structure was the same, and the tiny framed paintings, pillows covered in dust on each bed, miniature toys—were incredible. It was the nicest dollhouse Benny had ever seen. "But where is the next riddle? Or a letter from Evelyn?" she wondered. "I sort of thought when we opened the dollhouse, it would be sitting in here."

Zara scratched her head. "So did I. Maybe she was worried a kid would break into the house and find the letter, so she hid it in one of the little rooms?"

"But where?" Benny wondered, running her fingers along the walls.

"This is pretty nice for a toy," Ryan observed. "Did Evelyn or her kids even play with this thing?"

"Probably not. Listen to this," Zara said, her face illuminated by her phone screen. "Dollhouses before the nineteenth century were *not* toys. They were called 'cabinet houses,' and they were showpieces that were meant to flaunt someone's wealth." She clutched her phone to her chest. "God, my grandmother would be so impressed with me right now."

Benny's heart started to beat faster. "There has to be another letter in this dollhouse that I was meant to find." She shined a light on each little room, looking for something that could hold a letter or journal entries. She searched each little painting and looked at the small books on the tables, wondering if there was anything written in them. *Evelyn, what do you want me to see?* she asked herself, moving from the kitchen to the dining room to the sitting room to the library. She ran her finger along the tiny books on the shelves, feeling for anything that could resemble an opening, pressing on each bookshelf. Suddenly one sprung open like a door to reveal a narrow opening behind it, just wide enough to hold an envelope and a cloth pouch. Carefully, she used her fingers to pry out a small bag.

"That looks just like the satchels in those paintings we just found," Ryan said.

"It does!" Benny agreed. "There was a pouch like this in Evelyn's self-portrait in the library too."

"What is that stamped on the front of the pouch?" Zara asked peering at it. "Is that a bird?"

"It's a sparrow," Benny said, her skin tingling. She looked at Zara. "That is Evelyn's nickname. Her friends called her that because she was quick as a bird."

Zara held up her arm, and lightning flashed in the window behind her. "Goose bumps. Hang on. I'm going to go check those paintings again."

"Bring them over here," Benny told her as she opened the pouch. She pulled out a folded envelope, her heart pumping hard as she read the familiar handwriting on the front:

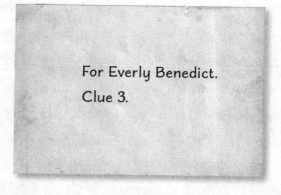

For Everly Benedict.
Clue 3.

If one clue was exciting, the second was even more so, and this envelope would lead her to the third piece of the puzzle.

But how many pieces were there? Would she have enough time to find them all? Benny tried hard not to think too far ahead, but with this game, it was hard not to. So much was at stake. And there was so little time.

You can do it, Guppy. She heard Grams in her head, and she steadied her breath. She was doing it. She was playing to win. This was big. She was one step closer to making Evelyn's and her dreams both come true. Her hands started to shake as she fumbled with the pouch to see what was inside.

Out came a heart-shaped charm on a thin silver chain. The chain and pendant were tarnished beyond recognition from years of storage, but Benny could make out a large *A* written in cursive on one side. She spun it around to see if it had a hidden compartment. "It looks solid. I don't think it is a locket."

Zara hurried over with the paintings. "Look! A girl is wearing a necklace just like that in this painting, which was also painted by Evelyn. It was with the other ones."

Benny shined a light on the canvas. It was dated 1850 as well. The girl had long curly brown hair and gray eyes that stared directly at Benny from the painting. She was standing on a sandy beach under clear skies, her white dress billowing in the breeze, and her expression was playful. In her hand was a familiar satchel. Benny flipped the painting over. This one had a name written on the back. *Agatha Bishop*.

"I wonder if this is the Aggy Evelyn writes about. Aggy is her best friend."

Zara stared at it a moment, seemingly lost for words. "Bishop. I know that name. I've heard Grams mention it before. I think we're related to the Bishops!"

The three of them were silent for a moment, taking in the strangeness of that revelation.

"Okay. I just got chills. If I'm related to the girl in this painting, that would mean..." Zara started to say.

"That you're part of this story too," Benny realized.

"What does the letter say?" Ryan prodded. "Is there another riddle?"

Benny had almost forgotten. She carefully opened the envelope. Inside were several additional pages from Evelyn's journal. There was no letter, but there was a new riddle.

If there's a light you cannot sea
When wild storms come along,
Trust your compass and promise me
You'll seek the siren's song.
If you do not hear the sea maiden
You must listen even harder—
Her burden was so heavy-laden
For he loved her with such ardor.
Where she lives now is lonely and bright.
I watch it from my window at night.

Benny looked at the others. They seemed to be trying to decipher the poem like she was. *Siren*...was she talking about a mermaid? A female pirate?

"Can I see the handwriting?" Zara asked, and Benny handed her the riddle. "Okay, this is interesting—she spells *sea* S-E-A for the ocean. That has to be on purpose. She also mentions a sea maiden and a siren."

"Mermaid?" Benny guessed. "Are there any famous mermaid statues in town?"

Ryan and Zara shook their heads.

"It was worth a shot."

"What does she mean by *Where she lives now is lonely and bright. I watch it from my window at night*?'" Ryan wondered.

Benny read the line again and, something inside her

clicked: "If Evelyn wrote this, then she must mean her balcony! Come on!" she said, hurrying downstairs and nearly running into Wally, who was carrying laundry. The others quickly followed.

"Are we in a rush?" Wally chuckled as Benny ran by him.

"We need to get to Evelyn's room," she yelled, excited.

"Don't you mean your room?" Wally teased.

Benny ran for the double doors to the small balcony, her heart thumping as she ran into the pouring rain and her eyes found what she knew for certain Evelyn wanted her to find. She pointed it out to the others. "*I watch it from my window each night,*" she repeated from the clue as the others reached her. "Evelyn wants us to go to the lighthouse!"

ENTRY 6

*From Evelyn Terry's Private Journal,
Dated June 7, 1825*

> Due to the Cough, school was
> canceled, and Papa forbade us from
> leaving the farm. But I was restless.
> I couldn't stop thinking about Aggy.
> Would she survive the Cough?

Aggy was very ill. I knew that from listening in on Papa and
Mama's conversations. They tried to tell me otherwise, but I
knew my friend was very sick, and my last words to her were
said in anger. I longed to see Aggy and apologize for things I
didn't understand, but Papa wouldn't let any of us leave the

homestead. Alone, I felt tortured. I hadn't taken the necklace that Aggy'd offered or taken the letter that afternoon, when I fetched her mother to help Aggy get home. We hadn't spoken since.

For the time being, our own household had been left unscathed by the Cough, and Papa wanted to keep it that way. For that reason, Papa made the journey to town alone to get updates and supplies. Two more families we knew had taken ill, school was not reopening for the week, maybe longer. Mama kept me busy helping her cook and clean. We sent a meal to Aggy's house, but her mother and aunt wouldn't let me past the front gate to leave it. *Will she live?* I wanted to ask them. *What was in that letter she wanted me to read? She's my best friend. I can't let her die.*

I refused to think of a world without Aggy in it.

There had to be a way for me to save her.

Captain Kimble, I decided, was the key.

I told Mama I was going to go for a walk to check on our grapevines. Instead, I heeded the call of the island, in search of Kimble and some answers. Despite the fog and dreary mist in Greenport, the second I cut through the brush near the shore, the island showed itself to me. I ran across the sandbar, feeling the warmth of sunshine return as I reached the other side. This time, I could see the fort clearly from the beach, and I prayed Kimble would be there.

The second I neared the fort, the vines pulled themselves away from the entrance, allowing me inside. Kimble wasn't there. My eyes flickered to the chest in the corner of the room.

If I wasn't mistaken, I could hear whispers calling to me from that trunk. I'd never seen anything like it, and to this day, it is a feeling I cannot properly describe. I couldn't look away. I felt drawn to that chest like a magnet—whispers beckoning me to come closer. Drawing near, I could see the carvings appeared ancient, like the chest was built in another lifetime, the gold filigree on the detailed scrollwork chipping away, the wood warped, the metal accents bent. Curiosity was killing me. What kind of treasure was kept inside that box? How did it keep Kimble young?

I stepped closer to the trunk, desperate to open it. *Leave*, a voice in my head told me, and I did, fighting my urges and retreating to search the island instead. I found Kimble emerging from the waterfall that guarded the cave.

He didn't look surprised to see me.

"Sparrow, I thought I told you to steer clear," he said, dropping a sack at his feet.

He was soaked from head to toe, and he shook his hair out like a dog.

"You remembered my name," I said brightly. "I came back because I had questions."

I heard him groan. "More questions? Kid, can't you see I'm busy?"

I rushed over, careful not to fall into the pool of water. "What are you doing? Can I help?"

"No." He opened the sack, taking out a pickax and some other primitive tools. Papa had far better ones. "You shouldn't be here."

"Shouldn't, but I am." I couldn't waste time getting to the point. "I need your help. My friend is sick."

He sighed heavily. "Poppet, I know what you're asking—"

"I didn't ask anything yet," I mumbled.

"Look, I can't even help myself." He looked up at me, his blue eyes reflecting the waterfall. "Get out of here, kid, before the island doesn't let you go."

My eyes welled with tears. "Please. I think she's dying," I said desperately. "I have to save her."

He stood up and faced me now. He was so much taller than I was. Taller even than Papa. "Sparrow," he said quietly, "you do not want whatever you think this life is. Not for you. Not for your friend."

"But—" I started to protest.

"*No*," he said, his tongue sharper now. "I won't let another person succumb to the same blasted curse that took me. It stole Grace! It took my crew! It's claimed too many lives already! Go on now, kid. Find another way." He turned me in the direction of the beach. "Get out of here while you still can. The Blood Orange Moon is days away, and then all of this"—he waved his hand around—"will up and vanish when it's ready."

"What do you mean, 'all of this'? Do you mean the island?" I asked.

He didn't answer me. Instead, he packed up the tools again and threw them back in the wet sack. "You heard me, Sparrow. Get out of here."

I thought fast. "You haven't found the missing piece yet, have you?" It occurred to me then that the missing piece was from the treasure chest. A coin maybe, or something gold. Without it, the treasure wasn't complete, the way it had been when he'd first stolen it.

He turned his head ever so slightly. He was wearing that thick, ridiculously heavy leather jacket again. It hung to the back of his knees, which were covered with high boots. Entirely inappropriate for the weather, yet he didn't break a sweat.

"I can help you search for it," I blurted out. "Show me what you're looking for, and I'll help you find it on the island. In exchange for saving my friend's life."

His face scrunched up now, and it was the first time I saw him angry. "This isn't a game, kid! No deals! If I can't find the coin in this maze of an island, you sure as hell won't be able to either!"

"I—"

"GO!" he thundered, pointing toward the beach.

I started running then, both angry and upset at the same time. Kimble needed my help! Why couldn't he see that? As I ran across the sandbar, I knew I would make him see reason. I had to.

EVELYN'S ISLAND

IMP DATES:

- Island supposedly disappeared: June 10, 1825—last Blood Orange Moon
- Next Blood Orange Moon: June 12, 2025
- DEADLINE to finish game: June 12, 2025!!!

What happened to Captain Kimble's treasure?

- Jonas Kimble born 1620. Died ???
- How does the Rudd family play into this?
- Why does Elias Rudd blame Evelyn for Axel's disappearance??

Evelyn's friends:

- Aggy Bishop (best friend)
- Axel Rudd (friend/enemy?)
- Gilbert Monroe
- Thomas Lyons
- Laurel Henderson
- Cat: Winks

CLUES:

- Evelyn's journal pages
- Small satchels—why does she use these?
- Why did Evelyn hide Aggy's pendant?
- IS THE LIGHTHOUSE THE KEY TO FINDING THE ISLAND?

SIXTEEN

BENNY

PRESENT DAY

The rain only got worse. The meteorologist called it a very early tropical storm for the season. High winds snapped power lines, brought down trees on roads, and caused the lifeline of Wi-Fi to be on the fritz. Ten inches of rain fell in two days. People canceled their reservations at the inn, unable to get the east end of Long Island by car, train, or even helicopter. Local travel was tough too, with Benny's mom sticking close to home to be with her rather than Harris, who she said was busy dealing with leaks and flooding at his area businesses.

Getting to an offshore lighthouse was out of the question in this weather. Benny could see the whitecaps on the water from

Evelyn's room, the sky so thick and gray, Benny wondered if they would ever see the sun again.

Not till after the Blood Orange Moon, she thought. *Which is in three days.*

Three days.

Three days to get to the next clue waiting in the lighthouse and whatever clue came after that. She found herself cursing the fact Evelyn hadn't numbered the riddles—what if there were ten more? What if there were twenty? She wouldn't make the deadline if that were the case.

Benny tried to focus on the new journal entries. She'd received two more with this riddle, giving her insight on Captain Kimble's immortality, the treasure that seemed to keep him young—that he was itching to get rid of—and the island itself. Benny was starting to believe there was a reason the island had never been discovered. What if it only appeared every two hundred years around the Blood Orange Moon? It didn't seem logical, but neither was a fountain of youth. So if the island only appeared every few hundred years, did that mean it was out there right now if Benny only knew how to find it?

She wished Evelyn would tell her. She hadn't written a letter with this clue, just the riddle. To try to make sense of it all, she'd written out Post-it Notes with all the information she had so far. Maybe she was missing something.

"Knock-knock," Mom said, coming and standing in her doorway. Benny knew immediately from the way she was dressed (silk top, heels, earrings, and her "fancy" jeans, as she called them), her mom was on the way out. "How's it going?"

"It's not," Benny said slumping down on the four-poster bed she loved way too much and burying her head in the expensive pillows. "I'm stuck."

"You? Stuck? Never." Mom sat down beside her and rubbed her back. "What's the issue? I thought things were going well."

"They were," Benny told her pillow. "But now the weather is working against me." She wanted to be honest: *I am so stressed out over finding the next clue in time so that we can keep this house and everything that comes with it that I'm not sleeping, and I don't know how to tell you that because you look the happiest you've ever looked and Harris seems good for you, but I'm scared this is all going to disappear in three days like Evelyn's island, and I can't fix this.* But she couldn't.

"I can't change the weather, but I can cancel my plans." Her mom rubbed her back. "Whatever it is, we can figure it out together. Remember what Grams always said when we had a problem?"

"*You know more than you think you know,*" they both recited.

"I'll cancel," Mom decided. "The weather is too awful for a

lunch at a fancy restaurant anyway. We were going to Hooked. Have you heard of it? Harris is a part owner."

"Really? I though the Rudds owned it."

Mom shook her head. "I don't think so. Harris said he had a stake in it."

Benny sat up. "How many restaurants does that guy own?" *Ryan must be rich*, Benny thought.

"Five," Mom told her. "But he said Hooked is the finest one. They apparently have a burrata dish on the appetizer menu that is to die for. But I can have it another time." Her mom's smile faded. "I know time is running out to finish Evelyn's game. I should be here helping you, not going out on dates, pretending I have a different life."

Benny felt her heart constrict. *Three days. Three days. Three days to win the game and find the island.* Could she do it? Would having Mom here help at all?

Just then her phone buzzed:

ZARA: SOS! Get here ASAP! I've got intel!

It was followed by an address. Intel?

Aggy.

You know more than you think you know. Maybe Grams was right. Had Zara figured out what happened to Aggy? Would that help them find the island? "You should go to lunch," Benny decided. "But can you drop me off somewhere on the way?"

"Of course," her mom said her smile returning.

Twenty minutes later Benny's mom was pulling up in front of a blue Victorian house with a wraparound porch a few blocks away from Greenport's main street. The paint was chipping off the shutters, and the porch looked worn but inviting, with a swing, potted plants, and a sign that said, *GRANDMA'S RULES APPLY HERE.*

Zara flung open a loud porch door as Benny got out of the car. "Get in here already! You need to hear this!"

Zara was waving her in like she was trying to medal in a track race. She had on a band concert tee that she'd frayed at the arms and cut jagged lines into the waistline of. Since they'd seen each other two days prior, she'd also drawn tattoos on her right arm. They looked like a map.

"Come on. Come on. You have to hear this. Grandma? GRAMS? Where are you?" Zara called, walking into the house ahead of her. The house smelled like cinnamon and had the air-conditioning on full blast. Benny rubbed her arms to keep warm. Loud jazz music was playing in another room.

"You call your grandma Grams too?" Benny asked, thinking of her own grandmother.

"Yes. Was your Grams also into listening to Alexa at full volume and obsessed with reading every biography ever written?" Zara asked.

"Yep. They might be the same person," Benny said, and Zara smiled.

"Alexa! Stop!" Zara shouted.

Benny heard Zara's grandmother groan as she came shuffling into the room wearing a turtleneck sweater. "Zara, I may let you keep your phone in your room at night, and buy you unlimited Oreo packages so you can sample every flavor even though your parents told me not, but I thought we agreed you wouldn't shut off Alexa on me." She saw Benny, and her expression brightened. "I see our museum explorer is back."

"Her name is actually Everly Benedict, but she prefers Benny," Zara explained, helping her grandmother to the sofa. "Tell her what you told me. Tell her!"

Her grandmother pursed her pink lips. "Stop shouting at me and fetch the family Bible. I'll show her."

Zara did as she was told, bringing over a very old-looking book with frayed edges. She placed it in her grandmother's lap. Her grandmother put on reading glasses.

"The Agatha Bishop you found a portrait of in Evelyn Terry's attic is one of our ancestors," Zara's grandmother told Benny. "She is the daughter of Alice Bishop, an only child whose mother later remarried and had another daughter, also named with an A. Her name was Abigail."

"Tell me that is not weird?" Zara asked Benny, her brown

eyes ablaze. "That you're related to Evelyn, and I'm related to Aggy, and we both met right before the next Blood Orange Moon?"

It is weird. Is it a coincidence or something more? Benny wondered.

"What's the Blood Orange Moon got to do with any of this?" Zara's grandmother demanded.

Benny and Zara both stiffened. "Nothing," they said in unison.

"Show her the Bible," Zara pressed her grandmother.

"Zara, really, I told you these things aren't an exact history," her grandmother huffed, opening a very old leather book that looked like it had been stitched back together more than once.

"Just show her," Zara insisted.

Her grandmother sighed. "Every birth, death, and important union in our family history has been recorded in our family Bible," her grandmother explained to Benny. "But unfortunately, in Agatha's case, only her birth date was recorded." She flipped through the records till she found Agatha's name and pointed it out. *Born April 18, 1812.* The date she died wasn't written down.

Benny noted all the other names and dates on the page. Only Aggy's didn't have a death date. "Why didn't they enter date she died?"

"As I told Zara, they simply could have forgotten to record

it. And then perhaps the knowledge of when she died wasn't passed down to the next generations," Zara's grandmother explained. "I did some digging of my own and found town records, one of which listed Agatha as having died of pertussis in eighteen twenty-five. Hundreds of residents died that June. They called it the Cough back then, but its real name is whooping cough."

"Evelyn left me pages from her journal, and they mention people getting sick, including Aggy," Benny told her. She couldn't believe Aggy died. Evelyn must have been devastated.

"Whooping cough could wipe out a whole town in those days," her grandmother said. "Medicine was hard to come by and expensive, and there was no known cure. Many sought out alternate treatments." She smiled. "I'm proud to say Zara and my ancestors—Agatha's mother and aunt—were healers, practicing homeopathy and eclectic practices. They helped the community back then. Many women practitioners did the same, but the Bishop family was known for being a tad unusual in their treatments."

"People thought they were witches," Zara said, her eyes sparkling with mischief. "Because they didn't understand their methods."

"They were not witches." Her grandmother tsked. "They just used methods not known to most at the time." She pursed her lips. "Though I have heard talk in our family that the Bishop women had the gift of sight."

Benny felt her heart start to pound. Evelyn talked about Aggy having the gift of sight. That's why her and Aggy had fought too, because Aggy saw something happening with the Blood Orange Moon and she wouldn't tell Evelyn what it was. Just that she'd be leaving soon. So did that mean Aggy ran away? Or had she known she was going to die of pertussis? She thought again of how Evelyn thought Kimble was immortal. "Is it possible Aggy didn't die from whooping cough?" Benny asked cautiously.

Zara's grandmother looked pensive. "It is certainly possible. Public records were written by hand, and mistakes happened." Her grandmother patted the Bible. "Which could explain why her death at that time or in the future isn't recorded here."

Benny thought for a moment. Axel reported missing. Aggy's death shrouded in mystery. Aggy's gift of sight. She had a feeling this all had something to do with the island. Benny felt her heart beat faster. *You are going to go on a big adventure, Guppy*, Grams said, and she'd been right.

Things were coming together in a way Benny couldn't begin to describe, like whispers on the wind. It was the game, but it was more than that. She could call it fate, call it luck, but the things that were happening were no accident. She owed it to

Evelyn to see it through. Reach the end of her story. The lighthouse was the next step. "Thank you for sharing this with me."

Zara's grandma smiled. "I hope it helps with the project you're working on."

Benny looked at Zara quizzically.

"For summer extra credit," Zara said pointedly.

Benny caught on fast. "Yes, it does," Benny said with a smile.

Zara's grandmother rose. "Now, if you'll excuse me, I have a date with Alexa to listen to Miles Davis." She raised an eyebrow at Zara. "And I'll listen at any volume I want."

"You and Miles have fun," Zara said. "Benny and I are going to visit the lighthouse."

Her grandmother's eyes flashed. "No, no, no one is going out on a boat out in this weather. We're in the middle of a tropical storm!"

"*Remnants* of a tropical storm," Zara reminded her. "We'll be fine."

"You sound like your parents, who go off in pursuit of pirate lore and leave me here with teenagers who don't listen," her grandmother muttered.

"But, Grams, we have to go," Zara tried. "Benny's, er, project is due on the twelfth."

The sound of rain hitting the porch interrupted the conversation. It was pouring again.

"No one is going anywhere this afternoon by boat," Grams declared. "We may need a boat to get through this town if this rain keeps up." She looked out at the porch, now barely visible in all the rain. "I'm not even sure how we're going to get people to the gala at the lighthouse in this weather. If Vivian Rudd's hair gets wet on her ride over, I'll never hear the end of it."

Zara groaned. "Gramsssssssss, pleasssseeeee."

Benny put a hand on Zara's grandmother's arm. She had experiences with grandmas too, and arguing was never going to get them anywhere. "You're right. We'll go another day."

Satisfied, her grandmother headed back to the other room, where she promptly told Alexa to play Miles Davis at full volume.

Benny grabbed Zara's arm and pulled her out on the porch, where the air was warmer, sticky, and hot. "She's never going to send the historical society boat out in this. We have to get there another way."

Zara sighed. "You're right. Maybe we can hire someone down at the docks. The Crab, aka Ansel, is always doing private fishing charters. He's probably expensive though. Maybe Ryan can float us a loan. He's going to want to come with us anyway."

Benny felt odd asking to borrow money. "We'll tell him to meet us at the docks in the morning. And don't worry about the money. I've got a few hundred dollars saved for an emergency,"

Benny said. Normally an emergency constituted rent. Food. Gas. But if they found this island, she wouldn't need to worry about those things or where Mom's next paycheck was coming from. "Hopefully that will be enough. One more thing." Benny pulled Aggy's pendant out of her pocket. "I think this belongs to you. After all, you and Aggy are family."

"No." Zara shook her head. "What if the charm is a key to the game and you don't know it yet? Keep it." She smiled. "Till you win the game."

Benny smiled now too. Outside, the rain was stopping. "Till I win the game," she repeated, and that's when she heard a meow.

In the walkway was an orange tabby. It stared at Benny intently, watching them, seemingly listening to their conversation. Benny had a sudden chill.

"Hey, is that the cat from the docks?" she started to ask, but when she turned back to point the cat out to Zara, it was already gone.

SEVENTEEN

BENNY

PRESENT DAY

"Where is he?" Zara barked, pacing the dock the next morning, sounding more anxious than Benny did. "We said ten a.m., didn't we? If I can get Grams to let me out of helping her at the museum this morning, the least he can do is be on time."

"I'll text him again," Benny said. She did and saw bubbles pop up as if Ryan was typing back; then they disappeared. Weird. "We'll give him another ten minutes; then we try to get a ride to the lighthouse without him while this weather holds."

She looked up at the sky, which was an inky gray, big puffy clouds rolling across the sky as if they were running away. *Please don't rain. Please don't rain. I've got two days to finish the game and find the island. I'm running out of time.* While the remnants of a tropical storm had passed, the air was still thick and humid, and the meteorologist said more rain was in the forecast along with high wind. At the moment, it was just a breeze, and the water was only a little choppy. Benny had a strong stomach. She could survive a bumpy ten-minute boat ride to get the lighthouse. Unfortunately not everyone was in agreement on boating in this weather. Most of the boats on the dock were not going out. Even the card-playing older guys from the other day weren't sitting on their boats in this weather.

"We can't wait. It could rain any minute," Zara decided, pulling up her hood as it started to mist. "I don't see anyone else out here today. We are going to need to suck it up and ask Ansel. He's probably the only one on his boat on a day like this. I swear, I think the guy lives on the water."

"Hopefully money talks and he'll take us," Benny said. If there was one thing she'd learned over the years, it was that money was a good motivator.

Benny and Zara headed to the end of the dock, keeping their heads down as the wind picked up. Benny snuck a glance at the aging fishing boat. She could see a figure in a black hoodie sitting at a table on the deck.

They were still several feet from the boat when they heard him yell down. "Whatever you're selling, I'm not interested,"

Ansel said, not looking up. "Magazines, those foul candy bars, a ticket to win a trip to Disney World, you can keep it all."

Up close, Benny sized him up. He looked a few years older than her mom. He seemed both world-weary and young at the same time. If she wasn't mistaken, the same orange tabby cat from the other day was sitting on his lap, watching Benny with interest. But what really caught her eye was what was on the table in front of him. Scrabble.

"We aren't selling anything," Zara said. "We were hoping for a ride to the lighthouse."

"We can pay," Benny added.

"Lots!" Zara added, shrugging at Benny. "Right?"

"I'm not a taxi, kid, and either way, the lighthouse is closed during the week. And I'm not going anywhere in this weather. Especially to the lighthouse."

Benny couldn't place his accent—was it American? Or British? It seemed a mix. "You don't have to stop the boat," Benny yelled up to him. "You can toss us over, and we can swim." She thought she saw a hint of a smile make a brief appearance. "Or you can just pull up, and we'll jump off?"

"As tempting as it would be to toss two annoying kids overboard, I'm in the middle of a game." He waved them off. "Now go away."

Benny stood on her tippy-toes and glanced at the letters

on his board. "If you use the *A* and the *F* on your board, you can add a *P* and a *J* and make *flapjack*. It's worth twenty-six points. And you could make at least fifty other words with that one word, you know."

At this, Ansel looked at her. His eyes were bright blue. "Not bad. Thanks, kid."

"No problem." Benny felt a flash of something familiar in his eyes, like a memory. She had the feeling like she'd seen his face before. She shook her head. Evelyn's story was making her second-guess her own. Benny held up several twenties. "A hundred dollars for a ride to the lighthouse?"

"Two hundred!" Zara seconded. "Three!"

Benny nudged her. "Hey. Stop giving away my money."

"Sorry." Zara shrugged. "I felt like an auctioneer for a moment."

"Kid, I don't care what you offer." He glanced over his shoulder at the choppy water. "I'm sticking close to land today."

"Please." Benny wasn't beyond begging. "You don't understand. We have to get to that lighthouse today."

He put down a Scrabble tile and looked at her. "Listen, kid, I'm going to teach you a valuable lesson that is good to learn early in life: the journey is more important than the final destination."

Benny froze. She'd heard that advice before. Those exact

words were written in Evelyn's journal. "In this case though, it's all about the journey. To the lighthouse," she tried.

He sighed. "Go. I have a game to finish." He scratched the stubble on his chin and stared at the board again, clearly done with this conversation.

Coincidence or not? She tried not to overthink it and focus on the problem at hand. It was no fun playing Scrabble alone. She'd done it. No wonder Ansel looked miserable. The cat jumped off his lap, sat on the edge of the boat, and stared at Benny again with its one good eye.

"Winks!" Ansel growled. "Get back here."

Winks. Just like Aggy's cat, who had one eye? Benny asked herself. But then she shook the thought away. Winks wasn't a completely unusual name for a one-eyed cat. She was grasping at straws again.

"Come on. We'll find someone else," Zara said. She started to walk away, annoyed.

Benny wasn't ready to give up. "What if I could make it five hundred dollars?" she tried. She noticed him hesitate. "Not a bad deal for an hour's work."

He chuckled to himself. "Don't take no for an answer, do you, kid?"

"Never," Benny said fiercely.

He looked at her then, his gaze was steady, and Benny

noticed a diamond stud in his left ear. Benny could almost see his brain working. "Do I know you?" he asked curiously.

"BENNY!" Zara was waving to her from the other end of the dock. She was standing with Ryan and Harris. "We've got a ride!"

"You snooze; you lose," Benny told Ansel and put the five twenties she actually did have on her back in her pocket before turning to walk away.

"Wait! Your name is Benny?" he yelled after her.

"It's short for my last name—Benedict. Everly Benedict," she said, walking backwards for a moment, before she took off toward Zara in a run. "Bye, Captain."

She could hear him calling her name as she took off down the dock, but she didn't look back. She had places to be. They had a ride, and the lighthouse couldn't wait.

ENTRY 7
From Evelyn Terry's Private Journal, Dated June 8, 1825

I awoke to the sound of my mother crying...

Mama's cries carried through the house, yanking me from my sleep. I stumbled out of bed to find her. The sky was still dark, and I could hear the rain falling outside as it had every day this week. I found Mama in the kitchen sitting at our table.

"Mama? What is it?" I could see her tear-streaked face in the shadows. "Are you sick?"

"No, sweet girl." She opened her arms for me to come sit on her lap, which I hadn't done in years. I obliged, frightened. "We are fine. It's Aggy. Your father went by there last night to check on them and..." She hesitated. "She isn't doing well, dear. Her mother is ill now too."

"No!" I started to cry. "What is going to happen to Aggy?"

"We're going to pray very hard that they all get well, and the Cough stays away from our home." Mama brushed my hair off my sweaty forehead, the breeze almost nonexistent, even though the window was open. "That's all we can do."

No, it isn't, I thought. *There's something I can do.*

I could get them medicine. I knew Aggy's mom and aunt were healers, but if their treatments weren't working, maybe I could barter to get medicine for them from the mercantile. Once Mama went off to do her chores, I snuck out of the house and headed into town, praying Papa didn't realize I was gone.

"Sparrow!" Gil jumped off the mercantile porch, spotting me right away. He stood a short distance from me. No one wanted to get too close with the Cough. "What are you doing out here?"

"I wanted to see if I could barter to get medicine for Aggy. Gil, she's terribly sick," I whispered.

"I heard," Gil said, his eyes wide. "The Hendersons came

down with it this week too. I heard Laurel is too weak to get out of bed."

"No," I said, fighting back tears at the thought of losing Laurel too. "What about the Lyons family? Has anyone heard from Thomas?"

Gil shook his head. "No. Not yet. But I'm sure if they need medicine, they'll come here. I'll send word if I hear anything," he promised.

"Thank you. You're a good friend," I told him, and we stood and stared at one another for a moment, wanting to say more, even if we didn't know what it was. It was so good to see him.

Then I heard someone whistling. I turned around. It was Axel.

"No one is supposed to be on the streets," Axel told us by way of greeting, his dark eyes narrowing at the sight of us together. "We don't need the Cough spreading."

"Who put you in charge?" I asked boldly.

Axel puffed up his chest. "My father. He says we should all stay home till this clears. Otherwise, everyone in Greenport will be dead and buried."

I shuddered. "Don't say such things."

"You're scaring her," Gil told Axel.

"Why? It's the truth. The Cough comes on fast, and poor people don't have the money for medicine," Axel said with a smirk. "The Lyons came round trying to barter for some, but my father sent them away."

I felt a rush of anger. "How could you let him do that? Thomas and his family are our friends."

Axel's expression darkened. "Rudds don't give handouts. You two better stay well. Lord knows neither of your families can afford medicine either."

"Why, you lout!" Gilbert went to hit Axel, and Axel jumped back and laughed.

I pulled Gil back. "You're a horrible boy, Axel Rudd," I shouted. "Shame on you for not helping your friends when they need you."

"Rudds take care of themselves." Axel fixed his shirt, which Gil had yanked. "You two should head home and do the same."

"Go home, you rat!" Gilbert shouted after him. "Go—" Gil stopped talking, a deep, thick cough racking his body.

I stepped back in horror. "Gil. No. Not you too."

He covered his mouth with his sleeve, looking as anxious as I felt. "You go home now, Sparrow. I'll be fine. Pray we'll all be fine."

He was the second person to say that to me, but I knew we needed more than prayers now. We needed a miracle.

And I had a feeling I knew just where to get one.

* * *

For something so precious, Kimble left the treasure unguarded often. He wasn't in the fort when I arrived, still angry after my conversation with Axel. Instead, I found Aggy's traitorous cat curled up next to the treasure chest. Winks saw me and hissed.

"I'm doing this to save your owner," I told the cat, who glared at me with her one eye.

I couldn't worry about Winks. I had to move quickly. I was nervous Kimble would appear and catch me in the act, but I also knew if he was missing a piece of treasure, then he'd be off in search of it. While he hadn't said it outright, I was beginning to guess that he couldn't be free of immortality till every last piece of stolen treasure was returned to this chest.

And if he was only missing one piece, I was now stealing his chance.

He'll get another one, I told myself. *He's lived two hundred years as a young man. He can live two hundred more till the next Blood Orange Moon comes around. How bad can living forever be? I have to save Aggy and my friends.*

I could feel the treasure calling to me as I neared the chest, the whispers growing louder and more urgent. *Welcome, Evelyn Terry! Welcome home!* The island knew I was here, and it wanted me to take its treasure. Who was I to deny the island this when I needed its help? I knelt beside the chest and placed my hand on the lid's latch.

Don't do this, Sparrow, I could almost hear Aggy saying. *You don't know the price.*

But I do, I told the voice, sure it was my own, even if I always considered Aggy my conscience. *I need to save you.*

Winks' eyes were on me as I lifted the latch. I heard a sound like air being whistled through a gap in a window as I opened the chest.

A gasp escaped my throat as I stared at its contents. The chest was filled with hundreds of silver coins, shiny, gleaming, and sparkling like new. They were the most beautiful coins I'd ever seen. I picked up a fistful and let them fall through my fingers and drop back into the chest. Then I lifted a single coin and stared at it. There was heft to the piece that I turned over in my hand. Waves of the sea were emblazoned on the obverse side, the pillars of Hercules on the other. There were markings of letters on one side. An *E* stuck out like a sore thumb. Holding the coin in my hand, the whispers grew louder, the coin growing hot between my fingers. I quickly pocketed the coin in a small velvet pouch that I'd made with scraps of purple fabric. Then I took three more coins and placed them in the sack as well. Then I shut the lid fast, the whispers growing faint again. The island, it seemed, was satisfied with what I'd done. Winks, however, was not. The cat was clawing my dress now as I tried to tiptoe out of the fort.

"Shoo, Winks! Shoo!" I told the cat, nudging her aside as I shut the fort door behind me, then watched the ivy cover the door, hiding it from sight again.

"Looking for me?"

I spun around. "Captain Kimble, sir!" I said nervously.

He was drenched again, his sack slung over his shoulder. He dropped it on the ground. He sounded out of breath. "We went over this, kid. *Sparrow*. I don't need your help."

"Have you found it yet?" I asked, trying to change the subject.

"Would I still be here if I had?" he replied.

Winks started to meow loudly, and I could hear her through the closed fort door. Kimble and I looked at each other. He studied me. "You go in there?"

"I don't know how to get in," I lied. "I was just coming to see if you needed my help."

"You didn't actually *say* anything," Kimble noted, stepping closer. His blue eyes were fierce as he held my gaze. "You're not planning on doing anything stupid now, are you?"

The ground rumbled beneath our feet. Kimble was unfazed, but I jumped. "What was that?"

"The island," he said, sounding frustrated. "Just reminding

me how much time I have left before..." He didn't finish the sentence. "I don't have time for this. Go home, Sparrow," he said, turning around and heading back out into the jungle of trees that swayed in the sunshine. "And don't let me find you here again."

"Yes, sir!" I said, relief flooding my body. This time I listened, running over the sandbar, back into the heavy rain and fog of Greenport, and not stopping till I reached my house. Inside, I rushed upstairs to my room, and as fast as I could, I wrote four letters. One for Aggy. One for Gil. One for Thomas, and a fourth for Laurel. I folded each letter and placed them in small purple pouches I'd made with scraps of fabric. On each, I stamped my symbol: Sparrow. So they'd know it was from me. I placed a coin safely inside each one. Then I waited for the day to end, for darkness to come and Papa, Mama, and my brothers to go to sleep. That's when I would sneak back out. There was no time to waste. My friends were growing sicker, and the Blood Orange Moon was two days away. I needed to get these coins to my friends. Their lives depended on it.

EIGHTEEN

BENNY

PRESENT DAY

"Got us a ride!" Zara was standing at the other end of the dock with Ryan and his dad. "Why didn't you tell me what we were doing this morning?" Ryan asked Benny. "If you'd said we needed a ride, I would have asked my dad to take us. He has two boats."

"*Two* boats. You didn't even tell me you had *one* boat." Benny wasn't sure she would ever be used to this world.

Ryan shrugged. "You didn't ask."

"Forgive him, Benny," Harris said. He was dressed in jeans and a green polo shirt, the Terry Estate Vineyards insignia stitched onto the front pocket. "He means we *had* two boats." She saw an expression she couldn't read flicker across his face. "We just sold one, and we'll probably have to sell this one too."

He grimaced. "Running restaurants is expensive." His face relaxed. "But for today, this boat is ours, so I'm happy to take you out on it."

"Thanks for the ride," Benny told him. "I thought you were having lunch with my mom."

"I still am. We just moved our reservation. When Ryan told me you needed a ride to the lighthouse as part of the game, I wanted to help." He motioned to the pricey watch on his wrist. "Deadline is fast approaching, and we need you to win."

"Thanks," Benny said gratefully. At least someone knew what they were up against. "I really appreciate it."

"And it's a *free* ride," Zara added, glaring at the other end of the dock. "Who needs Captain Grump?"

"Captain who?" Harris asked, stepping off the dock and walking to the next pier. They all followed. "No matter. Let's get you to the lighthouse before it rains again."

The boat was situated on the next dock. It was bigger than Ansel's and the other boats Benny had seen in the slips. It had two levels and a huge lower cabin area that could be the size of her whole last apartment. In just a few minutes, Harris had the boat started, Ryan had untied it from the slip, and they were pulling away from the docks and heading into open water. Shelter Island was on their right, and in minutes, Greenport became a dot in the distance.

Benny held on tight as Harris navigated the boat over the chop. It was too loud to have a conversation with Zara and Ryan stuck close to his dad, helping him with various tasks. That left Benny to wonder what they were going to find when they reached the lighthouse. Would the clue be in plain sight? Would they have enough time to find it? She went over the riddle again in her head, thinking about the words that could mean something: *Sea. Siren. Maiden. Compass.* What were they looking for? But before she could decide, the lighthouse seemed to rise out of the water in the distance.

It looked like a house on stilts. The lighthouse was square, three stories, with a circular tower above it sitting on a bed of rocks in the middle of the water. The island was no bigger than the lighthouse itself and had only a small dock for Harris to pull up alongside. Benny didn't see any lights on inside, except for the one shining from the lighthouse tower, circulating like a beacon. Behind the lighthouse, large black clouds were starting to form, like a warning. Ryan jumped off the boat, tied it to the dock, then put down a plank for them to walk from the boat to the dock as Harris kept the boat idling.

"Don't take too long," Harris said, shouting to be heard over the wind. "There's a storm brewing again."

We'll try not to, she thought as she followed Ryan and Zara down the dock to a door at the base of the lighthouse, which

Zara opened with a key she'd "borrowed" from the museum. Inside was dark. All Benny could see was storage boxes. Even the staircase looked like it was under construction. Light from the upstairs windows showed them the way.

"Come on up," Zara said racing up the stairs to the next level. "I'll tell Earl we're here and not to tell my grandmother we visited and borrowed her keys."

"Who is Earl?" Ryan wondered as Benny followed them.

"He volunteers here every week," Zara said, reaching the second floor first. "Knows more about this lighthouse than even my grandmother."

Benny reached the top step. The lighthouse was one big room on this floor. A spiral staircase stood in one corner and a *Save the Lighthouse* banner hung on a wall alongside a portrait of what Benny could only assume was the old lighthouse keeper. There was also a nautical map of Long Island on one wall. Otherwise the room was sparse.

Where would Evelyn have hidden a clue? Benny stepped up to one of the large windows overlooking the water and stared out. Even from this distance she could make out Evelyn's brown-shingled house on the shoreline in Greenport.

Benny heard feet on loud metal and looked up at the staircase leading to the lighthouse lookout deck. "I talked to Earl, and he vows to keep our secret," Zara told them. "He wants to meet you two, and then he'll leave us alone. I'm going to warn you; he's a talker, but I'll try to keep him brief so we can start searching this place."

Benny headed up first with Ryan right behind her. The next floor looked like it was once someone's home and was now a museum. There was a coal-burning stove, a table, a bed, and a wingback chair, all situated on a rug in a roped-off area. Along one wall were framed maps, artwork, old news-paper articles, model ships, and a TV playing a story about a lighthouse on a loop. A grandfather clock with a carving of a lighthouse on the glass case ticked quietly in a corner. Benny longed to stop and explore the area, but Zara was hissing for them to keep climbing. Another spiral staircase took them up to the tower.

A loud clap of thunder shook the foundation.

"Oh, boy. My dad is going to want to get going already," Ryan said, sounding anxious.

"We can't leave now," Zara protested. "We have to solve the riddle. And besides, it's not even raining yet."

"Yeah, but—" Ryan started, and Zara sounded like she was going to argue.

Benny cut them both off. "Why don't I go up and say hi to Earl, and you two start searching?" She pulled the riddle out of her pocket and handed Zara the necklace. "Take these. Maybe you'll need the pendant or rereading the riddle will help you. I'll be back down as soon as I can."

"Don't let him talk your ear off," Zara said as Benny hurried up the stairs.

"Got it!" Benny whispered back.

The area was tiny, but offered a spectacular a 360-degree view of the harbor, Greenport's docks, and Evelyn's house in the distance. In the middle of the circular space, the lighthouse lamp, much like the one at the museum, was whirring and spinning, the light flashing out on the gray skies. Benny noticed the clouds were swirling and moving fast, the storm rolling in, a sheet of rain seemingly heading right toward them. She didn't know how much time they had.

"Welcome!" Earl said. He was hard to miss in the space's one lone folding chair. Possibly in his seventies, Earl was wearing navy captain's hat, a *Save the Lighthouse* T-shirt, and khaki shorts with white Crocs. "Welcome to the Greenport Lighthouse tour," he said on autopilot. "I'm Earl Spoodle, and I'm a volunteer with the Greenport Historical Society. Today, you will be embarking on a fun-filled tour of this historical—oh." He realized Benny was the only one there and looked surprised. "Where did Zara go?"

"Hi, Earl," Benny said pleasantly as the wind whipped outside, making an eerie sound against the panes of glass. "Zara had to take care of something downstairs for her grandma, but she asked me to come up and say hello. I'm Benny."

Earl just looked confused. "Ben, you say?"

"Benny," she clarified.

"Benny," he repeated, committing her name to memory. Something caught his eye in the distance. "How did you get here? Does Thea know you're here?" He looked outside, and Benny wondered if he thought Zara's grandmother was going to drive up on a speedboat.

A flash of lightning made Benny ever more mindful of how little time they had. She heard something fall downstairs. "Well, it sounds like Zara needs help, but it was nice—"

"Can't leave without hearing me give my speech." Earl cleared his throat. "The Greenport Lighthouse was commissioned in 1850 by Evelyn Terry. It—"

"Earl, I don't know how long we can stay," Benny tried.

"It has been a working lighthouse ever since, though there isn't much need for one anymore in the harbor. Still, the Greenport Historical Society would like to see it be maintained. This place has always had an air of mystery." He leaned forward in his chair. "Did you know there are rumors about a tunnel leading from this lighthouse all the way to Greenport Harbor?"

Benny paused, intrigued. "Wait. Really? Is that true?" No one mentioned that before.

"That's what I heard," Earl said. "Been hearing that rumor since I was a kid, but it would make sense. You know, during the Prohibition Era, Hooked Restaurant ran a bootlegger business? It's true. Since the restaurant sits on the docks, small boats would pull up underneath. They had a trapdoor window that the ship would pass them booze through. The bar has a trapdoor behind it you can still see to this day. You ask that Ryan kid that Zara knows to see it. His family owns the joint. Anyway, there's a tunnel down there too. That one I've seen back when I bartended there in my youth. People were too scared to use the tunnel or see where it goes, but it felt like a good hiding spot if you ask me."

"Yeah, that would be," Benny realized, wondering now herself what else was down there.

"And if there is a tunnel there, makes sense it would lead here, but oh, what am I saying? People never listen to ol' Earl."

Another flash of lightning made them both look out the glass window. The wind was rattling the glass hard now. The clouds were closing in, almost as if they were overhead. A fog was rolling in over the bay. Benny noticed something strange. "Earl, why does the sky look green? Is that the glass or the light in here doing that?"

"Green?" Earl sat up and scratched his head. "It *is* green." He stood up and stared out at the water. "That's odd. It doesn't happen very often. In fact, I've only seen this happen once or twice before."

"What does it mean?" Benny asked. The wind was whipping so loud, she worried the glass might blow out. The sound reminded her of whispers. They sounded like voices.

Earl didn't seem to hear her question. His voice was barely a whisper as his nose smushed the glass. He sounded like he was in a trance. "It's the island trying to be found again."

Benny froze. "Did you say *island*?"

His eyes were like saucers as he stared at the horizon line. "Look out there. Can you see it? Hear it calling to you? It's the island waiting for someone to step ashore."

"You know about the island?" Benny inhaled sharply, goose bumps prickling her skin as she followed Earl's gaze out over the water, prepared to see nothing.

Instead, she saw it faintly, like an outline a person would sketch on a piece of paper—a small piece of land where moments before there was none.

Her fingers pressed against the glass, willing herself to be certain. *Evelyn's island. It's real*, she thought, heart pounding as she stared at the island, not far from the lighthouse, forested, with a small beach, and what appeared to be a fort, crumbling on one end of the shore.

It shimmered for a moment, almost like a mirage, before another flash of lightning lit up the whole tower, and then before she could even fumble for her camera to snap a picture, the island was gone.

ENTRY 9

From Evelyn Terry's Private Journal,
Dated June 9, 1825

> I told myself the island appeared to
> me for a reason. And that reason was
> so I could take Kimble's treasure to
> save my friends...

When I snuck out the next morning and reached Aggy's house, I saw the lantern already lit in her window, my best friend sitting up, waiting for me in the early dawn hours.

"Sparrow," she whispered. Her skin glistened, and her hair was matted to her face. I suspected she had a fever. The moment she spoke she started to cough. "What have you done?" She didn't seem angry at me, just resigned to her fate.

"I found a way to save you," I told her, getting as close to the window as I could. I was too eager to wait for her to read my letter. I wanted to tell her everything myself. "I brought you something. A coin from the island. From the treasure that made Captain Kimble immortal." Aggy started to protest. "Hush! The coin will make you well! But maybe you already knew that." I threw her the pouch.

She caught it and looked at the sack for a moment. Then she started to cough violently. "I can't see everything, Sparrow, just how it all ends." She was quiet. "That's why I wanted you to have my necklace. To remember me by."

"Remember you? You're not dying!" I insisted. "Open that sack! What's inside will save you. Hold the coin in your hand, and I'm sure it will work."

She pursed her chapped lips, neither telling me I was right or wrong with my prediction. Instead, Aggy opened the sack and held up the coin for me to see it.

I'm not sure what I thought would happen in that moment. How immortality would take hold of a person. But I expected something supernatural. A flash of light, perhaps, or for Aggy to give a gasp, and then her body would return to its natural pallor, her retching cough subsiding before my very eyes.

None of those things happened.

"Do you feel any different?" I asked hopefully.

Aggy hesitated, as if she knew something I didn't. "No. I'm sorry, but I don't." She started to cough again, drawing blood.

"I don't understand!" I couldn't help but sound frustrated. Overhead, I heard thunder. Mama would be looking for me soon in this weather.

"Why didn't it work?" I asked. Aggy didn't answer. "That coin is from Kimble's treasure chest. The one that made him immortal. I know it! I found it on the...island," I thought of something. "Maybe for the coin to work, you need to be on the island! Before the Blood Orange Moon." This had to be the key. Maybe this was how Kimble became immortal—he took the treasure when he was on the island, and now he remained immortal till all the treasure was returned. He hadn't found the missing piece, so he said, and now I had taken four coins he didn't know about, so there was still time to make this work. "Get to the island tonight! At dusk. I'll tell the others," I said. "*Promise me*, Aggy."

She gave a wan smile. "I'll promise, but only if you take the letter I wrote you."

"No," I said stubbornly. "I don't want to say goodbye. This is going to work! I can feel it."

"At least hold on to my necklace for me...until after," she

said decidedly. She passed the thin chain out the window, almost as if she had it ready, knowing I would come. She handed me the letter as well.

"Alright," I agreed, taking both, not wanting to be cruel. She dropped the necklace into my outstretched hand. "But I will give the necklace back to you. After tonight."

"After," she stressed. A flash of lightning made us both look up. "You should hurry and get the coins to the others before the storm."

"I love you, Aggy," I said suddenly. "You're my best friend."

"And you're mine, Sparrow," she said, tears filling her eyes. "And you always will be."

The rain started to fall as I walked away from her window, looking back to see her before I left. Then I hurried on, dropping letters to both Laurel, who was too weak to get out of bed, and to Thomas. He was in better shape than Laurel. When I reached his window, explained again what I had found and what he needed to do, he almost laughed through his coughing.

"Sparrow, this can't be true, but I'll try anything," he said, taking the letter. "And I'll see to it that Laurel gets there, even if I have to carry her myself."

I was feeling pleased with myself by the time I got to the mercantile to deliver the final letter to Gil. But that's when I realized I'd forgotten one detail—the mercantile wasn't open, a sign hanging on the double glass doors that said, *Sickness. Store Closed.*

Gil lived above the store. With the doors locked, I went around to the back of the shop, looking up at the second-floor windows, wishing more than anything Gil was sitting by the window. He wasn't. I looked around in desperation. Maybe I could hit the window with a rock and make him see me. I picked up a few small pebbles and started throwing. My aim wasn't great, but I managed to hit the corner of the window.

"What do you think you're doing?"

I spun around and saw Axel's father glaring at me, his hands on his hips. He was wearing an expensive suit with a pocket watch dangling from his breast pocket. Behind him, was Axel.

"I'm sorry, sir, but I need to speak to Gilbert Monroe."

"Can't you read, girl? The sign on the mercantile says it's closed due to illness. Go on, now." Elias Rudd tried shooing me away like I was a dog.

"I know how to read, sir. But this is urgent. I need to get this letter to him."

"What's it about?" said Axel, being nosy as ever.

"It's"—I thought fast—"a note from my father. For Gil's aunt and uncle."

Axel's dad just looked at me. "Slide it under the front doors. They'll find it eventually," he said before walking away.

"*Eventually?*" I felt tears spring to my eyes. I couldn't risk Gil not finding the letter in time. I needed to make sure he got my note.

Axel was still standing there, watching me. "What's the letter really about?"

I hated that he knew the truth. "Something that could help him get well, but I need to get it to him right away." The rain was faller harder now. "You must have a key to the mercantile. Just help me get inside, and I'll knock and leave it on their steps."

"They all have the Cough. No one is supposed to go in there," Axel said.

"The building isn't sick. I just need to slip the letter under his door. Please? Can't you do the right thing for once?"

Axel thought for a moment. "I can't let you in, but I can sneak in later and get the letter to him."

I was suspicious. "How do I know you're not lying?"

Axel looked at me calmly. "You don't. But do you have a better option? Other than breaking my windows?"

My windows. I hated when Axel talked about the building his father owned as it was his own. But he had a point about me being out of options. I needed to get this coin to Gil right away. I knew he would do whatever I asked of him.

I handed Axel the envelope. "Don't open it," I said, instantly regretting the words. I knew what happened when I told my brothers not to do something—they did the opposite.

Axel's eyes flashed from my hand to the envelope. "I won't."

"Maybe I'll just stand here till I know you've delivered it," I added quickly.

"I need to get the key from my father first and then slip away. He's not going to be happy if you're loitering around," Axel reminded me.

I heard myself sigh with frustration.

Axel awkwardly put a hand on my shoulder. "Sparrow," he said, using my nickname for the first time ever. "Don't worry. I promise I'll get this to Gil. Just go home and stay safe."

I blinked in surprise. Axel had never been that kind before. Maybe that was why I finally believed him. "Thank you," I said and started to retreat. "Guard that letter with your life," I added but didn't say what I really meant: *Gil's life depends on it.*

NINETEEN

BENNY

PRESENT DAY

"Benny!"

Benny heard Zara's voice and felt a jolt of reality grounding her. For a second, she was confused as to where she was. Then she remembered: Lighthouse. Storm. The riddle. But she couldn't shake the feeling she'd just seen something supernatural with her own eyes. Evelyn's island was *real.*

"Hurry!" Zara sounded anxious.

Benny turned to Earl. "Thanks for the...tour," she said.

Earl blinked too, staring at her as if she waking up from a dream. "Sorry? Oh. Yes. Tour." He nodded, his eyes still on the water and the greenish hue to the dark, stormy sky. "You're welcome. Please come back for our Save the Lighthouse gala on June twelfth."

"Thanks," she said. She gave the water—now choppy and churning, no sign of an island—one last glance, then rushed down the circular stairs. Zara and Ryan were arguing.

"My dad says we have to go," Ryan told her. "The storm came in out of nowhere, and we need to get back to port."

"But we haven't figured out the riddle yet, and who knows if we're going to get back here before the Blood Orange Moon?" Zara pleaded. "We can't leave."

Benny agreed, but she couldn't imagine Harris leaving them behind. "You haven't found anything?"

Ryan shook his head. "No maidens. No pictures of sirens. No compasses. Maybe we got this riddle wrong, and the lighthouse isn't the location of the next clue."

"We didn't get the riddle wrong! The answer is the lighthouse," Benny insisted as a wind gust seemed to make the entire lighthouse creak. "Evelyn commissioned this place, and I suspect she imagined seeing the island from her balcony." She looked around the dark room. "The clue has to be here somewhere."

"Then we have to stall Ryan's dad and find it," Zara decided.

Ryan's phone rang, and he pulled it from the pocket of the

raincoat he was wearing. He looked at the screen and winced. "It's my dad calling again. If I don't answer, he's going to come in here and drag us out. I mean it. We have to go."

"We can't!" Zara argued. "Benny only has today and tomorrow otherwise..."

"*Guys*," Benny interrupted, still feeling shaky after what just happened in the tower. "I saw the island."

Zara did a double take. "Wait. What? Where?"

"You mean it's real? Like really real?" Ryan asked, gaping as his phone started to ring again. "You're sure?"

"I saw it with my own eyes, and so did Earl," Benny told them. "It was there, and then it was gone...which means we're close. The entrance to the island has to be nearby." She glanced out the window again. "All this time I thought the island would just pop up like a mirage, but maybe the key to finding the island is knowing where the hidden passageway is to locate it."

"What do you mean?" Zara asked.

"If the island only appears every two hundred years, right around the Blood Orange Moon, then the reason we haven't found it yet is because we haven't located the spot where the entrance to the island is," Benny realized. "In Evelyn's journal pages, she talks about the entrance to the island being a sandbar hidden behind bushes, invisible to the naked eye. She finds it and shows her friends. What if it's the same now?

I saw the island when I looked out the lighthouse window. We're close, but not close enough to walk to it. We still need to find the secret passageway—maybe it's the beach, like it was for Evelyn, or maybe, since beaches grow and recede over time, there was a second way to the island, and Evelyn learned about the second way, and she's trying to lead us to the other path."

"But why a game then?" Ryan said, frustrated. "Why not tell you where the island is? Wouldn't that be easier?"

"I'm not sure. Her letters make me feel like she's afraid people might try to find the island for the wrong reasons," Benny told them.

Ryan ran a hand through his hair. "It's hard to know where the secret passageway is without reading her journal. Maybe there is something in those pages we would understand that you wouldn't. We're from here, you know.

"You might be right." Was she being a fool not to share Evelyn's private journals? She couldn't believe what she was saying about the island's location, but she believed it with her whole heart now. She'd seen too much not to. "I know this all sounds crazy, but..."

"No. It doesn't. If you believe, then maybe the island knows and that's why you just got a glimpse of it." Zara bit her lip. "Not sure why Earl did too, but..."

"So where is the island's entry point? Is it the lighthouse?" Ryan asked, peering out at the water. "If it is, why can't Zara and I see it too?"

"I don't know," Benny admitted. "And I didn't see the island long, so I'm thinking it's not the lighthouse. If it was, we'd see a way there, right? But we're close." She started to pace. "Earl told me there are rumors about there being tunnels from this lighthouse to the port. Something about a cave that they used to transport liquor during the Prohibition Era. And Evelyn mentions there being a cave on the island that they're too scared to explore."

Ryan frowned. "I've never heard of a cave, but there is a Prohibition room under Hooked. People like to go behind the bar and see the trapdoor they used to get downstairs and accept deliveries. Are you saying the entrance could have been there the whole time?"

"It could have been. But maybe it only appears around the Blood Orange Moon," Benny guessed. "Either way, if it is, there's something Evelyn knows we need to find here first," Benny glanced around the room. "We just have to find it." *Siren. Maiden. Compass*, she repeated. *Something has to be here.*

Ryan's phone rang again. "Okay, I can buy you a few minutes if I pretend to faint in front of my dad. I've done it before when he asked me to play pickleball." Lightning lit up the room followed by a loud crack of thunder. "I don't know how long I can stall, so hurry."

"We will," Benny promised as Ryan ran back down the stairs. She turned to Zara. "Tell me where you searched so far."

Zara clasped her hands together. "Okay, we've checked every painting. Every floorboard. Every dresser drawer. No sirens. No compasses. No maidens. Some of this stuff doesn't even look authentic. I think they are replicas of what they think would be in a lighthouse keeper's quarters. It can't be downstairs. They already cleared out that area for the gala. There's a pile of things stacked in the corner, but it looks like all lighthouse promotional material." She motioned to a child-size bed everything was crammed behind. A Save the Lighthouse poster was sticking out of one of the boxes.

Benny looked around—Zara was right. The space was pretty bare. She walked around, touching window frames, looking for seams that were in odd places, listening to the sound of the wind hitting the windows. Benny searched under the bed and checked behind a painting of the lighthouse again to be sure and came up empty. Frustrated, Benny kicked the boxes on the floor behind the bed. They fell over, pulling a blanket off something in the corner. Benny froze. "Zara? I think I found something."

Zara did a double take. "You did! That's a figurehead. My parents have one in their office, believe it or not. It's a seafaring tradition to have one on the front of the ship and that one is a—"

"Maiden," they said at the same time.

They pushed aside the remaining boxes and pulled out a large wooden carving of a woman. The paint was faint and chipping off her.

"I wonder what ship this is from," Zara said, her hands skimming the front of the figurehead. "My parents said pirate ships always had a carved wooden sculpture on the front of the ship to guarantee safe passage. They thought it was bad luck to travel without one. This one is old. Like really old. And definitely a maiden."

"Or a siren." Benny's heart began to beat fast again. "Think it's old enough to belong to a ship in Evelyn's era?"

Zara studied the markings on the carving—the woman was adorned with jewelry around her neck and a crown on her head. "If I had to guess, this is older. I've seen female ones lots of times, but see this crown? I've never seen one of a queen before."

This was it. Benny could feel it. Could something be hidden inside it? Benny knocked on the figurehead. It was pretty solid. She kept knocking on various locations till she came to the base where the woman's bare feet were, and this time, she could hear an echo. She peered closer. "Look! See that seam?" she said, excited as she rubbed her finger along an area that appeared to be glued. "This has been broken before."

"Maybe it broke and... Wait! You're not going to break it again. Are you? My parents would die. Benny, there has to be another—"

There was no time to debate this. Benny felt sick at the thought of what she was going to do, because if she was wrong—*Sorry Evelyn!*—she was about to destroy a piece of history. She picked up a black bird paperweight on the nearby desk and lifted it over her head.

"Wait!" Zara said, as the bird connected with the figurehead, sending wood pieces splintering.

Benny inhaled sharply when she saw the hollowed-out inside of the foot had a purple velvet sack and an envelope nestled inside. A black bird was stamped on the pouch.

""It's a pouch! Like the one in the paintings from the attic." Zara said, leaning over and staring at it.

"We found the next clue," Benny whispered. Her hands were shaking. She pulled both items out, being careful with the envelope, which was yellowed and fragile. On the front, as suspected, was her name, along with words that made her body tingle.

For Everly Benedict.

Herein lies your final riddle.

TWENTY

BENNY

PRESENT DAY

"The last clue," Zara whispered as the rain came, pounding the roof. "Evelyn said this is the final riddle."

"One riddle left," Benny whispered, almost to herself. "And one day left to play the game." Her heart was pounding now. "We have time to finish this."

I can still win this.

Another crack of thunder made them both jump.

"Benny! Zara! My dad is freaking out! We have to go!" Ryan called up to them.

"Coming!" Zara shouted. "Quick, let's put the figurehead back. Hopefully my grandmother won't notice it's broken till after the gala."

Benny pocketed the letter in her raincoat and placed the velvet pouch in her pocket. Then she helped Zara move the wooden figure back just as Earl descended the steps.

"Oh good, you two are still here. I'm leaving with you. This weather is wild!" Earl said. "Feels like we ticked off some gods or something."

Zara and Benny knew what the other was thinking. *Or something.* Like a Blood Orange Moon.

"Come on, Earl," Zara said, offering the older man her arm. "Let's get to the boat."

The boat was idling as they walked down the dock with Earl and helped him aboard.

"I'm sorry," Benny said when she saw Harris. "We were helping Earl with something that couldn't wait."

"Apologize when we make it out of this storm. Get inside with the others," Harris directed as Ryan untied the rope from the small deck. They pulled away from the dock quickly, the boat tilting and swaying in the waves.

Benny was sure she was going to be sick as Ryan held open the door to the large cabin and Earl made himself comfortable on a bed on the lower level. The older man immediately fell asleep, fears of capsizing in a storm obviously far from his mind.

"Did you find it?" Ryan asked hopefully. "Because if you didn't, I just pretended to faint for nothing."

"We got it," Benny said breathlessly, and pulled the satchel out of her pocket. She was desperate to see what was inside the pouch. Ryan and Zara watched as she opened the dusty pouch and a small round compact tumbled into her hand. The top of the compact was gold, burnished and tarnished from years inside a bag. Engraved on the top was a symbol that looked like a fancy star. "What is it?"

"I'm going to bet that's a compass rose," Zara said excitedly, gently picking it up and holding it up to the light.

"Compass! That was in the riddle," Benny exclaimed.

"It's a nautical symbol," Ryan added. "They're also called compass stars. They were used by captains to find their way on the high seas. Everyone owned one of these in the eighteen hundreds, whether they were seamen or not."

Benny took it back and looked at it closely, noticing a lever on the left side. She pressed it, and the compact popped open, revealing a glass dome and roman numerals. A magnetic needle under the glass held steady with the arrows up and down. "How does this work?" She tapped the glass and the needle started to spin. "Is this supposed to point north? Like it's directional?"

"Let me see," Ryan said and took it again, trying to stay steady in the bumpy cabin. He frowned. "Maybe you just thought the dial moved. This seems to be broken."

"Let me try," Zara said, taking it next. "Maybe you're doing it wrong."

"How can you do it wrong? You hold a compass, and the dial moves," Ryan said. "North, south, east, west. It's not hard."

Zara gave him a look. "Unlike working with sodium metal."

They hit a bump and collided.

"You are not bringing that up again, are you?" Ryan grumbled.

Benny reached over and took the compass from Zara again while they continued to bicker. Her fingers seemed to spark as she touched the warm metal. The needle immediately started to whir again, spinning lightning fast in circles in the palm of her hand. "Look!"

Zara and Ryan stopped arguing and looked over.

"Whoa. Let me see that," Ryan said, grabbing the compass again. The needle stopped again. "Okay, that's weird."

Zara plucked it back. The compass was turning into a game of hot potato. When Zara held it, the needle didn't move.

Zara looked at Benny quizzically. "I can't believe I'm saying this, but I think this thing only works when you're holding it."

"That's impossible," Benny sputtered, even though a little voice in her head was telling her the same thing. She took the compass back and moved around the cabin, trying to keep her feet steady as the boat rocked. The needle started to spin again, moving in her hand. She felt her whole body tingling, whispers and voices invading her head. *Is this really happening?* she wondered. Benny felt both nervous and excited, and her pulse was racing. "I think it's trying to give me the location of the island."

"Ryan!" Harris's voice came from above deck as the boat started to slow down. "I need your help up here."

"I'll be back," Ryan told them, rushing out of the cabin. "Don't figure anything else out without me."

"Maybe the letter explains what the compass is for," Zara guessed.

"Yes, the letter," Benny said, having almost forgotten about it. She removed the thick envelope from her pocket and carefully broke the seal. Inside were numerous journal entries, another riddle, and thankfully, this time Evelyn had included a letter. It was dated 1850 like the other letters. She read it aloud, not waiting for Ryan, her hands shaking as she spoke.

Everly Benedict,

You're so close to winning the game now.

Can you feel the island calling to you?

Have you maybe even seen it?

I picture a girl, my blood, staring out at my island and wondering what to make of such a fantastical place. I myself did the same. The choices I made on the island are not necessarily the ones you will make, but I hope these new journal entries enclosed will explain what led to my decision.

Some have called me rash. There are those who loathe me for what happened that day. I've made my peace with all of it. I know in my heart I did what I had to do to save my friends—Aggy, Gil, Thomas, and Laurel. My hope is, once you read these new journal entries, you'll understand why I'd go to such lengths, including leaving my inheritance and creating a game for a girl not even born yet as of this writing.

One journal entry remains. When you figure out the final riddle, you'll receive the final pages. As I've said before, everything written in my journal is true, as hard as it is to believe. I've hidden entries separately for fear they'll fall into the wrong hands, but now that you are so close to the end, I suspect you'll understand my reasoning.

The island's treasure is both valuable and dangerous. In the wrong hands, it could be exploited. Lives have been ruined because of it. But now you have the chance to right my wrongs. The last riddle will see you through to the end. Get to the island and save my friends. I beg of you.

One more thing...if you meet Captain Kimble at the end of this journey, please help free him too. We've made our peace, and he's a good man who deserves not only to live, but to age, as I have. There is beauty in growing older. I see that now.

Godspeed, Everly Benedict, and thank you. For everything.

Your final riddle:

> Underwater is the final piece
> Needed for the curse to cease.
> In order to find it, down you'll go
> To somewhere Jonas Kimble knows,
> Through a tunnel with no way out
> Until it's time to take the route,
> And find the place where I once roamed,
> So you may lead my dear friends home.

TWENTY-ONE

BENNY

PRESENT DAY

Benny and Zara were both silent.

"Forget the riddle for a moment," Benny said, trying to process what she'd just read. "Is Evelyn saying what I think she's saying? Does she think her *friends* are alive?"

Zara was nodding her head up and down as if she couldn't believe it either. "Alive *and* on the island. *Trapped* on the island. Wait." She threw her right arm out and grabbed Benny's arm. "That could mean Aggy is there too, no?"

Benny got the chills. "Is that why her date of death isn't noted in the Bible? Did someone know Aggy was still alive?"

"All this time," Zara whispered, "waiting..."

"For two hundred years," Benny added softly. Two

hundred years trapped on an island. Was Aggy alive? Were the other kids Evelyn mentioned alive too? Why didn't the letter mention Axel? "They can't be. Can they?"

"I want to say no, but you said you just saw the island with your own eyes, and you also said Evelyn's journal talks about Captain Kimble being alive for two hundred years, so...maybe it is true," Zara said, sounding shocked.

"Her friends are alive," Benny repeated, realization washing over her. "If that's true, no wonder Evelyn went to such lengths to make sure I'd finish the game! She left me everything so that I couldn't say no."

"Who would? Look at what she's left you. If you find the island. And apparently save her friends." Zara placed her head in her hands and screamed. "This is bonkers! Bonkers!" She looked at Benny again. "And don't take offense to this—why you? I know you're related and all, but how did she know your name? Or that you'd be born?"

"I don't know," Benny said, staring at the journal pages in her hand. She froze when she read the entry numbers. "These journals skip entries again. Look." She showed the pages to Zara. "Remember how last time they jumped from two to four and we thought it was a mistake? Well, these are numbered five, six, seven, and *nine*. That has to be on purpose. Don't you think?"

"It is weird," Zara admitted. "Evelyn seems to think of every last detail of this game, but somehow she mislabeled her journal entries? No. I don't buy it. But where are the other pages?"

"I don't know." Benny's thoughts were coming fast and furiously. Why wouldn't Evelyn give her all her journal entries? "She also mentions me running into Captain Kimble. So he's still here somewhere? Does he know about me too?"

"Maybe? It sounds like it, but where is he?" Zara rubbed her temples. "This is a lot to process. A lot."

"*A lot* a lot," Benny agreed. "And this is all aside from the riddle. If we don't figure out the final riddle, we don't find the island."

"Which means Evelyn's friends stay trapped," Zara added, sounding freaked out. "If they're really there. If they're still alive."

"So many ifs," Benny said. When she started this game, she couldn't imagine more than the fortune being at stake. People's lives were on the line. She had to figure this out. Her stomach was swaying as if she was still on the boat. Was this really happening? She had to clear her head and stop worrying about the other journal pages. Evelyn had to have her reasons. "Let's talk about the riddle." She looked at the page again. "'In order to find it, down you'll go to somewhere Jonas Kimble knows.'"

"So that must mean it's somewhere off the island, right? Because how else would Kimble know what she's talking about if he hadn't been here?" Her eyes flashed. "Or wasn't *still here*?"

Benny couldn't even think about that part yet. "'Through a tunnel with no way out,'" she continued. "'Until it's time to take the route.' Do you think she's talking about Hooked? Ryan said they had a hidden Prohibition Era room."

"The Prohibition Era wasn't until the 1920s, but that doesn't mean the storage room wasn't there beforehand," Zara reasoned. "That building—like many of the ones on Main Street—have existed since the 1800s. I think Evelyn even owned that location at one point."

"So it's possible," Benny decided. "Maybe that's where an entrance to the island is. Maybe it leads from Greenport to the cave. Evelyn mentioned there was one on the island."

"And maybe when you bring that compass we just found to the room, during the Blood Orange Moon, the island will show itself again."

Benny couldn't believe what they were both saying. Outside, she could hear the wind picking up again. She heard someone cut the boat's engine. "We have to get behind that bar. Right away."

Zara googled the restaurant as the boat seemed to bump its way into the dock. "But we need to get inside when no one is there. Otherwise no one will let us down there. Later tonight after dinner service? Ryan's dad owns the place. Maybe he can get us inside."

Benny's skin tingled. "No. I know we included him in the lighthouse, but Evelyn keeps stressing for me to be careful who I share all this with. We should keep this next part between the three of us." She heard footsteps.

It was Ryan. His raincoat was soaked. "We made it back. Keep what between us?" Ryan asked suspiciously.

"We have to get to Hooked," Zara told him. "Benny thinks that might be the place the last riddle refers to."

"Hooked? You mean the island entrance is in my dad's restaurant?" Ryan said incredulously. "But...but..."

Benny cut him off. "There's more."

"More?" Ryan's eyes widened as Benny held out the riddle for Ryan to read. At the end, he looked up. "It sounds like Hooked, alright. But my dad will never let me back out tonight in this weather. He's still kind of mad we took so long at the lighthouse."

"But the Blood Orange Moon is tomorrow," Benny reminded him. "This can't wait." Lives were on the line here.

Thunder cracked loud overhead and Ryan jumped. "Can't

going to Hooked wait till tomorrow? They have dinner service tonight. We won't be able to get in till late anyway."

"No," Zara said stubbornly. "We go tonight. No matter what time dinner ends. I'll meet you there," she told Benny. "Sorry, Ryan. But if you can't get out, we'll have to go without you."

"Seriously?" He looked mad. "I just took a hit with my dad so you could find the riddle."

"There's too much at stake here!" Zara argued as she pushed up the sleeves on her wet shirt.

Benny whistled loudly and they both stopped. "No one is going alone. We're a team. We finish this together."

This last week with Zara and Ryan was the closest she'd come to caring about people the way Evelyn seemed to care about her own friends. Yes, the clock was ticking, and there was more at stake than she even realized. This was more stressful than asking for more time on their rent or helping Mom find a new job. It was worse than broken air-conditioning or playing Sal for a free lunch. The whole life that she was trying to build for her and her mom was on the line here. Evelyn's friends' lives were on the line here. She couldn't screw this up. She needed Zara and Ryan's help to finish this.

Be careful who you trust, Evelyn had said. But the words *Be careful who you hide yourself away from, Guppy*, rang in her mind too. It was something Grams said a lot too. Maybe it was

time she fully let Ryan and Zara in on the game. She was trusting her gut. She looked at Ryan.

"Please find a way out tonight. We could wait till the morning, but I don't think we should. If we're wrong, tomorrow is
our last day to get it right, and I have to finish this game. Now
more than ever." She looked at both of them. "I trust you two.
And *only* you two." She held up the journal pages. "As soon as I
get home, I'll send you everything I have so far to read. We can
see if there is anything I missed in these journal pages before
we get to Hooked."

Ryan grinned. "Seriously?"

"Yes," Benny told him. "I want to make sure I didn't miss
anything. I'm sure Evelyn would tell me to trust my friends."
Friends. The word felt good. She looked from Zara to Ryan. "I
can't finish this game without you two."

Ryan was quiet for a moment. "Alright. I'll find a way out
of the house. They stop serving dinner at nine. Ten o'clock?"

Zara nodded. "I'll be there."

"Ten o'clock," Benny repeated.

"That was some nap!" Earl said suddenly, scaring them.
Benny had forgotten the lighthouse volunteer had been on
board. "Thanks for the ride back," he added as he walked past
her and Zara to go above deck.

"Ryan!" Harris called down to him. "We need to go."

The three headed abovedecks. Ryan ran ahead to talk to his dad, and Earl was gabbing away with Zara as they headed off, huddled under an umbrella. Benny pulled her hood up to follow them, but then she heard someone call her name.

"Are you Everly Benedict?"

Benny turned around.

Ansel was standing on the dock staring at her. His hood was drawn tight around his head, and he was soaked from head to toe, but he didn't seem to care. "Is that your name, kid?" He sounded agitated. "Or isn't it?"

"Yes, that's my name," she said, getting wetter by the second. Ansel just kept staring. "Why? Do I know you?" She could feel the hair on the back of her neck prickle.

"I'm...not sure," he said strangely.

"Benny!" Ryan was waving to her from the parking lot.

"I've got to go. Bye," she said and ran off.

When she looked back, Ansel was still standing there in the rain, watching her go.

TWENTY-TWO

BENNY

PRESENT DAY

The thing Benny always loved about games was that there was always a resolution. A person won. Others lost. Occasionally the game ended in a tie, but the rules were always clear. Scores were kept. Riddles were solved. Obstacles were overcome.

But Evelyn's game wasn't like other games. This game seemed to be changing. As Benny stood on the balcony in her room watching the fog roll in, she tried to make sense of what Evelyn was telling her.

She looked back at her first letter again: *Save them. All of them*, she'd written.

Now Benny understood what Evelyn meant. Evelyn didn't just want her to find the island. She wanted her to rescue her friends. Aggy, Zara's ancestor, and the others—Thomas, Laurel, and Gil, maybe even Axel—who had been trapped for two hundred years.

Was this really possible?

I have to believe it is, she told herself. *Evelyn put her faith in me, and I can't fail her now.*

At first winning had just been for her and Mom. The security of this house, of Wally cooking downstairs, of the inn and vineyard providing financial security. After so many years of feeling adrift and packing and unpacking, her stomach rolling as she thought about rent payments, she wanted a place to call home. And money to make sure she'd always have that home. Maybe Evelyn knew—without even knowing anything about Benny's life—that Benny wouldn't be able to walk away from all this.

But now?

I have to find Evelyn's friends in time, Benny thought, watching lightning flash across the sky. *If they're out there. If I don't find them in time, they'll be trapped for another two hundred years.*

The question was, would the island reveal itself when she went through the tunnel underneath Hooked, having cracked Evelyn's last riddle? What if she was wrong? Benny sighed. Why hadn't Evelyn given her the final piece of the puzzle—her last journal entry? As of now, she had no idea how Aggy and the others went from receiving coins meant to save them to getting trapped on the island. Axel was reported missing, but why weren't Thomas, Laurel, and Gilbert? And where was Captain Kimble now? Was he on the island with them? Somewhere on Long Island? Or halfway around the world? Did it matter? Maybe finding Kimble wasn't the key to finishing the game.

"Why me, Evelyn?" Benny said, her voice carrying on the wind. "Why did you think I could win your game?"

She didn't expect an answer, but one would have been nice. Instead, a gust of wind blew the balcony door shut behind her. Benny opened it and hurried inside, watching as the wind blew her Post-it Notes about the game off her wall.

Her phone buzzed moments later, and she found herself in a group text with Zara and Ryan titled Operation Island. The two were freaking out over Evelyn's journal entries.

She doesn't care about the island. She did all this because her friends are probably ALIVE! Aggy is ALIVE! Zara wrote, while Ryan wrote, I can't believe this. Can you believe this? Do you know how much this treasure is worth if it's real?

Benny heard a knock at her door and found her mom standing in the doorway, hair in curlers, wearing sweats and a silk top. "This is some weather!"

"Yeah, the wind is really picking up," Benny told her.

"Wally left flashlights downstairs for us in case we lose

power," Mom said. "We have a generator, but it's always good to be prepared. I'm having dinner with Harris if the whole town doesn't blow away."

"Are you going like that?" Benny teased.

"Very funny," Mom said. "He's picking me up in an hour. We're going to one of his restaurants over in Southold. We were going to go back to Hooked, but he said the restaurant called and there was some flooding. They're not doing dinner service.".

Benny froze. Hooked was closed? She had to text the others. They could meet earlier.

Her mom's smile faded. "I thought it might be nice to get out tonight in case you don't...well, you know." Her mom's smile was sympathetic. "Peter called me this afternoon, and I wasn't sure what to tell him."

"He texted me," Benny said, her stomach twisting again at the thought of their lawyer.

She'd seen the text and ignored it till she got home. How's it going? Peter had written. Just checking in since the deadline is tomorrow and we will need to discuss further actions if the game isn't completed.

I bet Vivian Rudd's team is circling like vultures, Benny thought. I'm close! she'd written back. And she was.

But close wasn't enough. You have to win. You have to find the island. Should she tell Peter about the immortality and

Evelyn's friends' disappearance? *No*, she had decided. And she didn't want to tell her mom either. It sounded ludicrous, and it wouldn't help matters now. She had Zara and Ryan. "Don't worry. I told him I was close, and I would check in with him after tomorrow."

Her mom walked over and hugged her. "I'm not worried. No matter what happens, we have each other, right?" She looked at her. "Win or lose, I get to keep you, and that's all that matters. Who needs all this house and land anyway?"

Benny felt her shoulders tense. *We do. We would take care of this place and love it the way Evelyn did.* "I'm going to win the game, Mom. I know I can do this."

"I do too," her mom said, and pushed a strand of Benny's hair behind her ear. "So fill me in. Where is the island?" Her mom looked to the windows, where a thick fog had obscured the view. "Was it a tiny little island that was misnamed or something?"

"Something like that," Benny lied. She couldn't get into it now. She didn't want to risk her mom talking about this with Harris. He was bound to ask her tonight with the deadline tomorrow. She'd tell her mom everything later. "Ask me again after I've won."

She grabbed her phone and texted the others: Hooked closed early! Let's go NOW!

"Tomorrow then," her mom said, her voice sounding lighter. "I'll ask Wally to make us something extra special tomorrow to celebrate the fact we're staying!"

Benny felt her stomach swish. *I will win. I can finish this, Evelyn. For you and me and my mom and your friends.* "Yes," she said, managing to keep a smile on her face and not give away her fears. "We're not going anywhere."

TWENTY-THREE

BENNY

PRESENT DAY

The fog thickened by nightfall, making the short bike ride into town a bit spookier than Benny would have liked. Thankfully the rain had stopped for the moment, even as the wind picked up. The sky was practically orange as she biked through the wet streets to get to Hooked. The fog was heavier by the water, making it too easy to walk right off the pier into the fog without realizing it. She didn't even see Zara till she was right in front of her. She had her hood pulled up on her raincoat, flashlight in hand. The lights inside Hooked were on, but Benny didn't see anyone in the windows.

"Is Ryan here yet?" Benny asked, keeping her head down to keep warm. The wind whipped around them.

"No." Zara rubbed her arm to keep warm. "The last of the workers just left while I was standing here. I heard him say a pipe burst and flooded the kitchen."

"Really?" Benny asked. "I assumed the flood was from the weather."

Zara shook her head. "Nope. For once, something has nothing to do with the Blood Orange Moon. Unreal though, since Hooked just reopened this summer after an extensive renovation. How could a pipe break already?"

That is weird, Benny thought. It made her think of something Sal said to her at his diner back in Boston: *When business is slow, I think of flooding this place and collecting the insurance money.* Would Harris do something like that? Why would he need to?

Benny heard a meow and looked down. It was that one-eyed cat again. The tabby meowed at her feet, clawing at her sneakers. "You should not be out on a night like this," she said to the cat. "Go home." The cat sat down on her sneakers and looked up at her, its tail switching. Benny sighed. "Suit yourself."

"Anyway, what is bad timing for Hooked is good timing for us." Zara bounced on her toes. "If Ryan would just show up and we could get inside. I'm freezing, and it's going to pour again." A gust of wind threatened to topple them both.

"Did you try the door?" Benny asked. "Maybe someone is still in there and it's open."

Zara grinned. "Why didn't I think of that?" She tried the door, and it opened. The cat scurried off, and they hurried inside. A river of water soaked the hardwood floor, splashing as they walked. "Ryan? You here?" There was no answer.

That's weird too Benny thought. Where was he? Maybe she was just being paranoid. He was as excited about this next clue as they were. He'd show up. He was probably waiting for his dad to leave to sneak out.

Benny looked around. The restaurant's vibe was nautical and pricey. Hooked was one large room, with massive windows overlooking the water. The walls were painted navy and accented with paintings of sailing vessels and large artsy pictures of shipping knots. The flooded floors were a shiny mahogany. Someone had placed the chairs on the tables to prevent them from getting ruined. A stack of china dishes sat on the bar.

"What a mess," Zara said.

"If up here is flooded, do you think the room below is too?" Benny worried. There was the sound of rain again hitting the roof, followed by a flash of lightning.

They raced over to the bar. It looked like the front of a ship. Zara stepped behind the bar and shone her flashlight on the wet floor.

"Where's the trapdoor?" Benny sloshed through an inch of

water and spotted a rubber mat. She lifted it and saw a small gold latch over a square of wood. "Bingo."

"Are we going to go down there without Ryan?" Zara asked.

"I don't know if this can wait," Benny said. "He knows where to find us."

Zara dropped down behind her. "I've heard about this storage room my whole life. Half this town was built during the Prohibition Era, so there are a lot of these secret storage rooms."

Benny tried turning the latch and pulling, but it was so tiny, she couldn't get a good grip. "It must pull open, but not with this latch." She felt around the board, pressing her hand on different areas till she suddenly heard a click.

"You got it!" Zara exclaimed. The wood lifted a smidge so that Benny could get a grip on the panel and pull it open. Water rushed inside the opening and Benny prayed there wasn't more below. The wood creaked as she pulled the small door open and peered into the darkness below. The air smelled musty and damp. She clicked on her flashlight and saw a ladder. "I'm going down."

"I'm coming with you," Zara said, shining her light on the dark quarters below.

Thunder boomed, louder this time, a storm moving in as Benny started her descent. Zara was right behind her.

The room wasn't very deep. In seconds Benny was on the

wet ground. Thankfully there was only an inch or two of water down there so far. The air was much cooler, and the room was larger than expected, so much so that Benny couldn't even see the other end of it in the darkness. She shone her flashlight around. The walls were rough, as if they were chiseled out of rock, and it was deathly quiet, the sound of dripping water the only thing she could hear. Much of the space was empty, which worried her. What if they were wrong about the riddle? Zara came into view, her flashlight's beam shining in Benny's eyes.

"Sorry! I hate to sound like Ryan, but it is creepy down here." Zara shone a light on the nearest wall, and Benny saw wooden shelves, a few still with very dusty bottles on them. "Where is he anyway? It looks like no one has been down here in a while. Ryan!" Zara yelled up to him. "Are you here? This place is creepy!" The room echoed, which meant it was larger than either of them knew, but it felt like a tomb. Benny tried not to think about that fact.

"If no one comes down here, that's a good thing," Benny said, scanning the bottles, looking for something that might be out of place. She pushed a large cobweb out of the way. "That means no one found whatever Evelyn hid." *Where could you have hidden something important?* Benny wondered, her heart beating faster.

"Hopefully," Zara moved around the room. "If she put

something down here, then we have to hope a bootlegger didn't find it. This building may have been here when Evelyn was alive, but remember, afterward the Rudds bought it and people used to boat in under this pier to pass crates of bottles through a secret window."

"Why would Evelyn sell Hooked to the Rudds?" Benny wondered aloud. If they didn't get along, why would a sale like this even come about?

Zara's flashlight landed on a small window. "It doesn't make sense. They didn't trust each other, so why sell to them unless she had a good reason? Unless she was hiding something under their very noses."

"I wouldn't put it past her," Benny admitted. Evelyn seemed to think of everything. "Do you see a window anywhere? Isn't that what they used to take shipments?"

"Yes." Zara's flashlight stream moved around the room. "My parents said rooms like this existed even during the height of piracy, so there has to be one under here. Even in the 1800s I'm sure people were doing deals they didn't want anyone to know about. They'd use a secret password and knock to get someone to open the window and make the trade."

Where was the window? Benny spun around, searching in the darkness. "Which means the window has to be relatively large, right? If they were passing crates through? And it can't be underwater, but we are in a building on a pier, which means this room is probably half on land and half on the water..."

"We just need to find the wall that overlooks the water, and I'm all turned around down here." Zara spun around.

Benny tried to be brave and walk farther into the darkness to find the other wall. She walked slowly, until she hit a wall and shone a light on it. There was the window. "Found it!"

Zara hurried over, and the two shone their lights on the window frame. It was warped and splintering from years of neglect. Dirt and grime, cobwebs and spiders had taken residence in the glass panes, but it was there, a window out to the water that was just below the waterline under the dock. Benny's heart started to pound.

"Evelyn would have thought to place something in a wall that wouldn't be disturbed till my time so she might have thought a window frame in a hidden room wouldn't be disturbed," Benny guessed, running her hand along the wood, looking for something out of place. She felt a vibration in her pocket and thought it was her phone. She pulled the item out of her pocket and realized it was the compass. It started to spin wildly, then stop, its arrow facing the window. Benny inhaled sharply.

"Okay, that's weird, right?" Zara asked, her voice hushed.

"Very," Benny agreed. "I think something's here. Shine your light on the frame while I check this out."

Their beams crossed, and they slowly moved their lights down every inch of the frame till they came to a place on the left side that looked like a black smudge, splintered and chipping away. Benny peered closer. It wasn't a smudge at all. It was a stamp. Of a sparrow. "Look!"

"It's the same bird that was on the pouches in the clues!" Zara said excitedly. "I can't believe Ryan is missing this. Ryan! Where are you?" she shouted. "We think we found something!" She suddenly screamed. "Okay, something just ran past my feet."

Benny tried not to think of rats. "Ignore it! Something is behind this wood," she said, trying to focus as her heart beat faster. "Help me pull the frame away."

The two pulled at the wood around the window, struggling to get a grip, even though the wood was old. Benny turned around, found a bottle opener on one shelf, and tried to use it to pry the wood till a piece sprung free. She hammered at it, kicking up dust that made them cough. Finally, she heard a crack, and they pulled the splintered wood away. Benny couldn't believe her eyes. Her hands started to shake.

Inside was a familiar-looking pouch.

"Is that what I think it is?" Zara asked quietly.

Benny pulled the pouch out, her heart fluttering, her lips dry. The pouch had a black bird stamped on it too. Inside was only an envelope. She read aloud what was written on the front.

For Everly Benedict: Here enclosed is my final journal entry. Read this and finish the game. If I'm right, an entrance to the island should be here in this very room during the time of the Blood Orange Moon.

Get to the island. Save them.

Finish this, and do what I could not in my lifetime. I have faith in you.

Benny got the chills. Quickly, she broke the seal on the envelope with trembling hands and pulled out the final pages.

"Read them aloud," Zara said with urgency, shining her flashlight on the pages.

Benny held her own light steady and began.

ENTRY 10

From Evelyn Terry's Private Journal,
Dated June 10, 1825

For the first day this week, it didn't rain. Fog rolled in off the water, blanketing my father's crops and the ground, making it hard to see from my bedroom window...

The sky turned a strange shade of orange, and the wind picked up this afternoon, leaving the water with a constant chop, whitecaps on the bay. The air was thick like a blanket, both warm and cool at the same time.

My father stared at the sky. "The Blood Orange Moon has arrived ahead of schedule."

My heart thumped in my chest, panicked. "Can it do that?" I'd told my friends to be at the island at sunset. What if they missed their chance?

"The Blood Orange Moon can do whatever it wants, my dear girl," Papa said. "There will be a storm, I'm sure of it, and we will need to bring the animals in to give them shelter. I'll need your help."

"Yes, Papa," I said softly.

I hugged my father then, which made him laugh. "Well, isn't this a surprise?"

"I just want you to know how much I love you," I said, breathing in the scent of fresh cotton that he always wore thanks to Mama doing the wash. I kissed Mama too and tried not to get emotional as I rubbed the head of our dog, Walter.

I didn't know if I was coming home again.

It was the one thing I was struggling with. If my friends took Kimble's treasure and could live forever, how could I grow up and grow old without them? They'd stay young while I eventually withered away.

Selfishly, I wanted to save them and be together.

But if I had a coin, and I left with them (because we'd

have to leave town, wouldn't we? How would we explain why we stopped aging? We couldn't.), I'd lose my family, who I loved desperately.

Did I go back to the island and steal another coin for myself? Or did I keep my feet firmly planted on dry land?

I walked down to the water to contemplate my choices, and the island revealed itself to me once more. I could hear the treasure calling to me, but I didn't heed its call. I just stared at it, like a mirage and wondered what future me would decide. *Where is Kimble?* I wondered. *Does he know what I've done?* If he did, he was surely angry with me. My betrayal affected him too, and the guilt was eating at me.

Hours later, I still hadn't made my choice. I snuck out to meet my friends at the sandbar at dusk. I was the first one there, holding tight to my cloak as the wind whipped through the trees and the thunder rumbled. Rain was imminent, but on the island, I knew it would be sunny and warm, as always. Whispers called to me from the other shore. *Welcome, Evelyn Terry! Welcome!* I tried to ignore them and focus on the path, willing my friends to appear.

When I saw Aggy approaching, my heart sung with hope. "Aggy!" I said, running toward my best friend.

She held up her hand to stop me, coughing hard and trying to catch her breath. Her face had hollowed in just a few days, the dark circles under her eyes worsening, and she was wearing a white nightdress. "Don't come closer."

"It's alright," I said. "You won't be sick much longer now. We need to get you to the island. Then the coin will work. I'm sure of it."

"I believe it will," she said, sounding terribly sad.

She was staring at me as if she was trying to commit me to memory, but in that moment, I knew my decision. I wanted to be with my best friends. With Gil. With Laurel and Thomas. All of us would be together: A family, like we were on this isle of forever.

"Don't be sad," I begged, wishing I could hug her. "I'm not going to leave you. I've decided. I'm coming too. I'll steal one more coin from Kimble's treasure and join you. We will be young. Forever. All of us together as we're meant to be," I could hear my voice shaking, my hesitation possibly seeping through.

That could be why Aggy shook her head then and smiled sadly. "Sparrow, listen to me," she whispered, starting to cough again. "I can't stop what is already in motion. What's meant to be will be, but what comes after is up to you." Her eyes searched mine. "You're the only one who can save us in the end. Did you read my letter?"

"No," I said stubbornly. "I don't need to. We aren't saying goodbye. You're going to be fine!"

Aggy's eyes were sad. "I just wish you'd read my letter. So you'd understand. I don't want you to be angry after..." She sighed. "Just know I am not mad at you. You're like my sister."

Mad? I didn't understand what Aggy was trying to tell me. "We are like sisters," I agreed. "That's why I'm coming with you."

What I didn't tell her was that while I had made my choice, I was scared too. I didn't want to leave my parents, my brothers, or Greenport, but I couldn't let Aggy go through all this alone. Why did my friends get sick while I was spared? Why did I have to choose which life I wanted to lead?

"You can argue with me, Sparrow, all you want, but we both know you can't come with me. Your path is different than mine!" she said forcibly now. "I explain why in my note. Promise me you're going to read it."

I pulled the envelope out of my pocket in anger and made a move to rip it up. "No! You don't get to decide my future for me! Why should I grow old when you all get to stay young together?"

Aggy snatched it and held it out of reach. "No," she said. "I won't let you be a stubborn mule. This letter is important and you will want it later."

I started to cry and Aggy hugged me. I was so surprised, I

let her. "I'm sorry," I sobbed. "I just don't understand why you don't want to be together forever."

Aggy was calm. "It's not that I want to leave you. It's that I have to." Her lower lip trembled. "You've always been stronger than me." I tried talking and she shushed me. "You have! That's why you have to do what's hard and stay behind now. If you really care about us, you'll do as I say. You know I have the gift of sight. You have to trust me on this, even if it doesn't make sense." Her eyes searched mine. "Promise me you won't come to the island tonight. You'll let the treasure be. You've done your part. Now let me do mine. Promise me, Sparrow. As my best friend, you must swear. On your life."

Aggy never swore. This was serious. "I promise. Just tell me why? Please. You owe me that."

Aggy smiled then. A real smile. "Because I want you to live. And grow old. And marry someday, have babies, and name one after me. You aren't sick. You and your family will be fine. And you will be too. You are going to have a wonderful life."

I let out a sob. "How can my life be wonderful if you aren't in it? We won't be friends if I grow up and you stay the age you are now. When you come back from the island tonight, you will have changed and I will still be the same."

Aggy's eyes had a sparkle to them. "Actually it is the

opposite. You are the one who will do many things," Aggy told me. "You will play many games, but this one, the one in my letter, is the most important game you will ever play. You aren't in this part of the story. We need you to be here. In Greenport. That's how you save us." She clutched my hands now, despite her illness, and started to wheeze. "I know you don't understand. But you will. After. And..." She hesitated. "Be patient with Kimble. Don't hate each other for what happens. You will need each other. Promise me you'll find a way to get through to him someday. Promise, Sparrow."

"What happens to Kimble?" I asked, but before she could answer me, I heard shouting.

Gil was coming now, followed closely by Thomas, who was carrying Laurel. She looked worse than anyone, but she was alive and clinging to Thomas's neck.

"We're here, Sparrow," Gil said, smiling at me despite how ill he looked. He was pale. So very pale.

"You came," I said, wiping my tears and placing Aggy's note back in my pocket.

"How could I not when you said we needed to be on the island for the magic to work?" Gil replied.

"I still don't understand," Thomas said. "How do you plan on saving us?"

"Only medicine can help me now," Laurel whispered,

leaning her head on Thomas's chest. "I don't mean to scare you, Sparrow, but I don't think I am going to make it."

"Don't talk like that," Thomas said, his voice hoarse. "Sparrow has a plan. She found this island, didn't she?" He started to cough, unable to finish the sentence.

I couldn't handle hearing Thomas like that or seeing any of them so ill. Aggy could barely stand, but her eyes never left my face. For someone about to be saved, she looked so sad.

"I did, and now you must go," I said. "Quickly now. Take your coins and get to the island. I think the magic needed to make you well only works if you're there."

Gil looked at me blankly. "What coin?"

"The coin," Thomas said, and held his and Laurel's up. "Didn't you get one?"

"No," Gil said worriedly.

"Yes you did," I insisted. "I placed it in your pouch. There was a letter and a coin inside. A piece of eight."

Gil pulled his envelope from his pocket and frowned. "My envelope had no such coin, Sparrow. Just a letter."

Everyone looked at one another as thunder rattled the earth.

"But that's impossible! I gave Axel the envelope to give to you. He promised he'd give you what's inside. He—Axel." I realized something and looked at Aggy. I could tell from her face she already knew. I could feel myself pale, my legs starting to wobble, threatening to take me down. Axel had done just what I'd feared he'd do. And I'd told him everything he needed to know about finding a treasure that could make one live forever. He'd even taken the coin I'd earmarked for Gil to help him get well. How could I have been such a fool?

There was no way the richest boy in town was going to allow our friends to be richer and live forever without him. I knew then what Axel would do if he found the treasure chest. He would take it. All of it. And sell it to the highest bidder.

How much would someone with the Cough pay to be well? To live forever?

That rat. Why had I trusted him?

"I gave you each a coin to take to the island so its magic would work before the Blood Orange Moon was high and you could be well again. That coin is the key to saving you. It will let you live forever." I closed my eyes in horror. "Axel must have taken your coin. He's going after the treasure for himself."

"Look!" Thomas cried pointing to the island visible from the sandbar. Lights appeared in the growing darkness. They had to be coming from a lantern. *Axel.*

"We have to stop him," Gil instructed. "A treasure like that is too powerful to be in the Rudds' hands. They will squander it. We have to get it first!"

"Come, Gil!" Thomas said, angry now. "Let's go get your coin and protect the treasure. Aggy? Can you get Laurel to the island?"

"I can," Aggy promised as Thomas passed Laurel off to Aggy, and she leaned on Aggy's shoulder. "Go. Hurry!"

"Oh Aggy, what have I done?" I said, starting to cry again as I looked at Laurel, so limp. "I should have found a way to get Gil his letter. I shouldn't have trusted Axel. If Gil doesn't get a coin in time..."

Thunder sounded loud overhead, and the rain began to fall. Laurel winced as she tried to lift her head. Then she started to cough again.

Aggy reached for my hand. "Gil will get a coin. Everything is going to be okay, Sparrow. But I have to go now and get Laurel across to the island."

"I'll help you carry her," I said.

Aggy's brows furrowed. "No, you have to stay here. You and Captain Kimble."

"Kimble is here?" I asked, alarmed. "He left the island? But I thought he couldn't till he found the missing coin."

Aggy pursed her lips. "He is searching in many places. There is more than one way to get on and off the island."

The cave. The one we were all too fearful to explore. I had seen Kimble emerge from it before. Where did it lead?

CRACK! A bolt of lightning hit a tree nearby, startling us both.

The thunderclouds were pulling in closer, blocking the moon. When I looked up, the sky started to darken to purple, snuffing out the light. The Blood Orange Moon was here. There was a rumble beneath my feet as I stood on the sandbar halfway between my world and the island's. I wasn't sure what was happening.

Aggy started to cough then, hacking so hard, she pulled out her handkerchief. I could see the blood begin to spread through the thin cotton fabric. Laurel, by comparison, had closed her eyes. If it wasn't for her chest rising and falling, I'd think she was gone. Aggy was right. They had to go now.

"Go," I said. "Hurry! Take Laurel and get to the island. I'll see you after it's done."

The rain pelted the tops of our head and hit the water like darts. It came down in sheets, the water growing choppy and so dark, I could hardly see. Aggy propped up Laurel and slowly helped her start to cross the sandbar.

"Get to the shore," Aggy yelled back. "And please read my letter." I started to protest. "This is important. Don't tear it up! And take care of Winks for me. Promise me you'll look after her."

This time I didn't fight her. "You're speaking as if I'll never see you again. You'll be right back." Aggy's expression was hard to read. "And I wouldn't worry about Winks. She manages fine on her own. I even found her on the island with Kimble one day."

"You did?" Aggy looked surprised. "That's...interesting. Now go. Hurry to the shore. I love you, Sparrow."

The words got caught in my throat. "I love you too, Aggy." The ground started to rumble again, and I ran in one direction as Aggy and Laurel went in the other.

"Nothing can keep us apart forever," she shouted, her voice growing farther away now. "Not even a Blood Orange Moon." Her eyes flashed as lightning lit up the sky again. "Remind Kimble: another moon will be here—in two hundred years."

I wanted to tell her that she'd be the one who would be alive to see it. Not me. But I didn't want to argue. Right now what was important was that she get to the island. Two hundred years seemed so far away. The rain was coming down so hard now that I couldn't see my island. But I imagined I was there with the others. The sun shining on my face as I pictured them holding small pieces of eight in their palms, their fevers and coughs subsiding, the color coming back to their faces. And then they'd walk back across the sandbar, different but the same. Them frozen in time at the ages they are now, me burdened with continuing to grow older.

But they'd live. That was what was most important.

The eclipse slid closer into view, and the world was blocked out, the darkness so threatening, I felt it might swallow me whole. I ran for shelter under a large tree as the storm raged, and waited to see them come across, healthy and new. It felt like they were gone forever, but there was no sign of any of them. I already missed them. The rain stopped suddenly, and I reached into my pocket for Aggy's letter, curiosity finally getting the best of me. What could be so important that she had to write it down for me?

I opened it and stared at her words in confusion.

Her message didn't make sense. And the date was nonsensical. Had the Cough made her delusional? Was I reading this correctly? What did she mean?

Find Everly Benedict, age 12, June 2025.

She is the key to saving us all.

Aggy, I don't understand your letter, I thought, but when I looked back at the island for answers, it vanished from sight as if it had never been there at all.

"No!" I cried, but my voice wasn't alone. Someone else was shouting too.

I looked over and saw him standing there, Captain Kimble, his wet, muddy clothes clinging to his body as he put his head in his hands.

Uh oh, I thought and took a step backward. My foot snapped a twig and he looked up and saw me. That's when he growled, almost as if he knew.

"Kid," he said hoarsely, "what did you do?"

TWENTY-FOUR

BENNY

PRESENT DAY

Benny finished reading Evelyn's pages and stood in stunned silence. She stared at the last lines of Evelyn's final journal, the flashlights casting an eerie glow over the pages in the darkness. Benny's hands were shaking. "Aggy knew my name," she realized.

"That's why Evelyn picked you," Zara said, sounding equally amazed. "Because Aggy's premonition showed you being the one who could rescue them from the island. You're the curse breaker."

Benny felt woozy. "They needed someone who would be alive for the next Blood Orange Moon," she reasoned. "But there are other people in our family line who are still alive.

My mom even. Peter said she was disqualified because of her name change, but Aggy couldn't have known about *that*. Could she have? I still feel like there's something we're missing."

"We could be," Zara agreed. "We don't know why the journal entries are misnumbered. We don't know where Kimble is now. Or where that treasure even came from."

"There's so much I still don't understand," Benny said, frustrated. "I don't get how Aggy knew my name. Or why *I'm* the one."

"Maybe you'll never know," Zara said gently. "But it is you, and now you have to finish this. For Evelyn, but for the others too." Zara shone her flashlight into the darkness. "If the island is out there and one of my ancestors is on that island and alive. And my age? And she predicted your birth? She's badass."

"Badass and smart, because really she was saving Evelyn, wasn't she?" Benny decided. "Evelyn got to live a whole lifetime, and create an inn and an estate that is huge today because she got to grow up. And Aggy...if she's out there...on this island... is frozen in time with the others. And maybe Kimble. Stuck in a time she won't recognize if...we find her." They had to find her in time. Benny's heart twisted and turned like cotton candy being spun at a state fair. "We need to get to the island."

"I'm coming with you," Zara said decisively. "Aggy is my family. I can't leave her to—AAAH!"

She started screaming and banged into Benny, who did all she could to keep from dropping the journal or her much-needed flashlight in the water.

"Rat! Big rat!" Zara was shouting. "There is something down here!"

Benny felt something run across her feet and screamed now too. She used her flashlight to scan the ground, looking for something small and slimy to freak out over even more, but instead, she found herself staring at two yellow eyes in the darkness. They were too large to be that of a rat or a spider. "Hang on. Shine your light by mine."

Their beams crossed again. There, sitting in the middle of the floor, was the cat that had been outside Hooked.

"It's a cat!" Zara sounded relieved. "Wait. How did it get down here?"

Benny's fingers tingled. "It looks just like Ansel's cat, who—and don't freak out—I think is named Winks."

"Winks as in the same Winks that is Aggy's cat? The one she told Evelyn to look after?" Zara asked, staring at the cat. "You don't think? It can't be. Can it?"

Benny stared, and the cat seemed to stare back, its tail flicking in the darkness. "Winks?" The cat's eye seemed to widen with recognition. Then it sauntered over and sat on Benny's sneakers again. She felt a chill go down her spine as the cat lifted a paw and licked it as it stared up at her. It let out a small meow.

"This is mad," Zara said, freaking out. "This can't be the same cat! Winks? Is that you? Are you a good immortal kitty?" The cat meowed again.

Benny's hair was standing up on end. "If this is Winks, then she's getting on and off the island through the cave, which means the cave has to be down here in this room."

"But why can Winks come and go and no one else can?" Zara wondered.

"I don't know," Benny said. Suddenly she had more questions than answers. She looked at the cat. "Winks, do you know where the entrance to the cave is?"

There was a loud bang from above and the cat took off, her orange and white tail moving fast past them, then disappearing into the darkness. Benny and Zara followed the cat, walking for a few minutes till they found a wall.

"Where did she go?" Benny asked, pressing on the wall to see if it was a door.

Her hand shot right through it.

Zara tried to do the same thing. Her whole arm went through the wall. "What is happening? I see a wall, but we can put our hand through it? How?"

Both girls looked at one another, then took a step closer

at the same time. *This is it. I can feel it*, Benny told herself. Her hand was shaking as she stuck her hand out again and that's when the wall started to waffle, like a sheet blowing in the wind, and then a loud hiss filled the air. The wall disappeared, a gust of wind rushing through the opening and threatening to knock them both over, it was so strong. Benny and Zara blocked their faces as debris kicked up and pelted them, then abruptly stopped.

Everly. Everly Benedict, welcome!

Benny froze. "I just heard someone calling my name."

"Me too," Zara said, sounding alarmed. "It said, 'Zara Dabney, welcome.'"

Benny had the chills. "It's the island. It's calling us," she whispered and shined her flashlight at the opening. She found herself staring at what looked like a long tunnel. No, not a tunnel. A cave.

"This has to be the way to the island!" Zara exclaimed.

The compass in Benny's pocket was vibrating again. When she took it out, it was spinning madly. Zara shined a light on it, and the arrow stopped spinning and pointed north—toward the tunnel.

"I can't believe it! We found it," Benny said excitedly, noticing how the air felt warmer in the tunnel than it did in the room they were in. "This is how we get to the island!"

"What are we waiting for?" Zara asked. "Let's go!"

"What about Ryan?" Benny asked, suddenly remembering he wasn't there. "Shouldn't we wait for him?"

"Don't bother. I'm here," Ryan said, stepping out of the darkness behind them.

"Finally! Where have you been?" Zara yelled at him.

There was something strange about Ryan's voice. He sounded tense. Benny looked at him. "Are you alright?"

Ryan didn't answer her. Before Benny knew what was happening, Ryan ripped their flashlights out of their hands. "I'm better than fine. I'm going to the island. Without you."

TWENTY-FIVE

BENNY

PRESENT DAY

Benny's heart thudded in her chest. Her stomach tensed and she almost knew what was happening before she even said it aloud. *Be careful who you trust.* She wasn't sure if she should laugh or cry. The first time she put her faith in someone else, they double-cross her. How did she not see this coming? "You tricked me," she realized.

Ryan's smile was eerie in the low light, the friendly smile she remembered nowhere in sight. "Took you long enough to realize it."

"Trick? What trick?" Zara asked, clearly not part of whatever Ryan was up to. "What is wrong with you, Ryan? Give us back our flashlights and let's find the island together."

Ryan ignored her and stared at Benny. "Thanks for finding the entrance for me." His voice was eerily calm and he didn't sound like himself. "The fact that it's downstairs at one of my dad's restaurants feels like fate."

Benny didn't understand how this had happened. "What do you want with the island?"

"You're smart, Benny. Don't make me spell it out for you. I'm sure you know what we want," Ryan snapped.

"*We?* The treasure," Benny said.

Ryan clapped mockingly. "See! I knew you were smart. Why else would I make sure my dad's restaurant was closed tonight unless I wanted to make sure whatever you found wasn't found by anyone else?"

"You flooded the restaurant," Benny realized. What a fool she'd been. She slipped the compass back in her pocket, hoping he hadn't seen it.

Ryan's face was hard to read. "Turns out sodium metal works well with pipes too."

"What is wrong with you?" Zara asked.

Benny studied him closely. Ryan's shoulders were tense; his expression was pained; he was even talking funny—all serious and angry. This wasn't the Ryan she'd come to know. Something changed. "Why do you want the treasure? Is your dad okay? Or is this about your sister?"

Ryan gave a disgruntled laugh. "You mean my half-sister? Who lives with my ex-stepmom? And I never get to see either of them." Pain flickered across his face. "All I have left is my dad and—" He cut himself off. "I need to do what I can to make things right between him and Vivian Rudd and finding that treasure is it."

"She's an investor in his restaurants?" Benny assumed.

"Something like that," Ryan said coolly.

"And your dad is in financial trouble." Benny had to keep him talking.

"Big trouble," Ryan confirmed. "My dad is in so deep, I heard him tell our lawyer he might have to take out a second mortgage on our house! On *our house*, Benny." He freaked out. "He sold both boats. He canceled our summer vacation. He has to pay child support for my sister and alimony for my ex-step-mom." His eyebrows furrowed. "I'm not losing my house because he is on this mission to prove—" He stopped himself. "He's the one who foolishly invested in too many restaurants that aren't working. I'm not losing the life we've built because of it."

Benny could almost understand his twisted logic. Ryan wanted to feel safe and secure, just like she did, but the treasure was messing with his head. Just like it had Axel's. The irony was eerie. "I understand where you're coming from."

"You do?" Zara and Ryan said at the same time.

"I do," Benny told Ryan, trying to remain calm. "I know what it's like to worry about money. About a house. How it feels to try to fix thing for your parents, but Ryan, this isn't the answer. If I win the game, I'll have the money to help you. And I will."

Ryan's face twisted miserably. "I don't want your handouts! I want my life to stay the way it is, and if I get the treasure, it can. He'll be so proud of me for fixing things with the Rudds," he said wistfully. "Then he won't need to keep investing in failing restaurants, or tell me there is no time for me to visit my little sister, or sit on the stupid Terry estate board of trustees—which doesn't pay a dime, by the way. We will get to keep the life we're accustomed to, and he'll owe it all to me."

"Ryan, you tool," Zara started shouting. "This isn't about some stupid treasure! There are people trapped on that island. *People*! And they've been there for two hundred years! My ancestor is one of them."

"What are you talking about?" Ryan demanded. "The last page I read of the journal said Evelyn gave Aggy a coin and it didn't work."

"There's more. The last pages of the journal were down here," Benny explained, pulling them out of a pocket. "Evelyn wrote that once her friends took the coins on the island, the island disappeared with them on it. We think that means they're still there. Trapped." Ryan just looked at her. "We think they're probably alive. Immortal. Like Kimble. And the whole reason Evelyn created this game for me was so that I'd save them."

"Even if Evelyn wrote that, you don't know that anyone is on that island," Ryan said, sounding more hesitant. "If the island disappeared, maybe they did too. Like Kimble. If he's alive, where is he, huh?" He shook his head. "No. The only thing I care about on that island is the treasure. That's what I need, and I'm going to get it."

"Ryan, listen to me," Benny tried again. She was so mad at herself for letting him into her world, but she couldn't focus on that now. She had to make him see reason. "It's not that simple. If you take that treasure, you'll be cursed, like it is."

"I'll worry about that later," Ryan roared, trying to push past her.

Benny and Zara blocked him.

"No!" Zara yelled pushing him back. "I'm not going to let you trap these people there another two hundred years by pissing off some supernatural island and taking its treasure chest."

Was that what would happen if Ryan ran off with the treasure? Or would he just be cursing himself? Truthfully, Benny didn't know enough about the treasure or any of this to know for sure. But Ryan wasn't thinking straight. "This treasure has to be returned to wherever it came from. But first we have to save Evelyn's friends. You're right—we don't know for certain they're there or they're alive, but Evelyn thinks they are, and I have to believe they are too. Don't doom them to stay trapped there. Read the last pages of Evelyn's journal." Benny held out the last pages.

"Please, Ryan," Zara now begged too. "We have to help them. Forget the treasure."

"Taking the treasure only leads to doom," Benny added. "The only chance we have to fix what happened is to rescue Evelyn's friends now, during the Blood Orange Moon. I don't know how long the tunnel will stay open."

Ryan stared at the pages a moment and stepped away. "I don't have to read them. I don't care what those pages say. I'm sorry. I need that treasure." He swayed slightly. "It's hot down here, isn't it?"

"Actually, it's much cooler," Zara noted.

"No, it's hot and I'm feeling faint," Ryan said, stepping back. "I—"

Benny heard a loud noise and then the sound of debris falling, water rushing into the hole and raining down on them. Benny and Zara clung to one another, trying to shield their heads. Something crashed through the floor above and a piece of ceiling landed on Ryan, who went down hard. Benny looked up in wonder. It was a man. He jumped up and dusted himself off, shaking Sheetrock out of his wet hair.

Benny inhaled in shock. It was Ansel.

He looked from Ryan on the floor to Benny and Zara, and groaned. "Kids. Great. Why is it that there are always kids in my way?"

TWENTY-SIX

BENNY

PRESENT DAY

Ansel picked Ryan up off the floor, which was now rising with water as it spilled in from the flood above. Ryan's eyes were closed, and his body was limp. Benny rushed over to feel for a pulse.

"He's okay," she told Zara, who reached down and retrieved their flashlights, shook out the water, and handed one back to her. "He's just knocked out." The beam glitched, going on and off. Thankfully the gaping hole above provided more light.

"Good. I'm mad at him, but I still don't want to see anything happen to the idiot," Zara mumbled.

Benny gave Ansel a look. "You could have killed him!"

Even in the darkness, she could see the deep blue of Ansel's eyes. He was dressed in a white short-sleeved tee, dark jeans, and combat boots. "Hey, kid, do you think it was my idea to come crashing through the floor? I went to the drop-down door behind the bar to get down here, and was looking for something to pry it open with when the floor just opened up beneath me." He hoisted Ryan onto his shoulder like he was a sack. "What are you three doing trespassing down here?"

"What are we doing?" Zara demanded. "What are you doing down here?"

He pursed his lips and shifted his weight to hold Ryan steady. "I asked you first," he said like a petulant child. "This room has been out of commission...for a long time. How did you even know it was here?"

"How do you know it's here?" Benny countered. Her flashlight came to life again and the beam caught Ansel's arm. Benny saw a tattoo peeking out of his T-shirt and felt a prickling sensation at the back of her neck. "Your tattoo. It's of a bird." She glanced at Zara. "It's a sparrow."

"Like the one on Evelyn Terry's velvet bags," Zara realized. "And like the one stamped on this window."

"How do you know who Evelyn Terry is?" Ansel demanded, stepping into Benny's flashlight beam. "You're her," he said, staring at Benny. "The girl from the docks yesterday. Aren't you? Everly Benedict."

"How do you know that? How does he know that?" Zara asked, freaking out a bit as water continued to rain down from above. It was now up to Benny's calves.

Benny's heart was beating out of her chest as she stared at him. The tattoo. His eyes—like Evelyn described. His hair. His age. The slight accent in his voice. The cat, Winks, who was his and yet Aggy's too. It all was too coincidental. "You're him, aren't you? You're Captain Jonas Kimble."

"No. He—*no*," Zara said.

Ansel, however exhaled through his lips, the sound like a whistle. "Now that's a name no one has called me in a very long time."

Benny had goose bumps. "You said that to Evelyn too."

He just looked at her. "And she said you'd come when it was time." He stared at her a beat. "And if you're anything like she was, kid, I'm not even going to try to argue with you." He hoisted Ryan higher. "So let's get going," he said heading into the darkness. "The island is calling us."

Benny and Zara reached for one another's hands and followed him into the darkness.

Benny's heart was beating fast now as she trailed behind Kimble in the tunnel. Did she call him Kimble? Or Ansel?

She'd call him Kimble, she decided. Benny shined her flashlight on him and saw him attempt to put Ryan down on the ground, still wet with water. "Wait! We can't leave him here. What if the tunnel floods? We have to take him with us."

"We do," Zara agreed. "Even after he was a total jerk. You have to carry him."

"Kids," he mumbled to himself. He hoisted Ryan higher and kept walking.

Benny was trying hard not to think about the fact that the man walking through the tunnel ahead of them was four hundred years old and looked the same age as her mom.

Or that she was about to walk onto Evelyn's island.

Where she'd hopefully find Evelyn's friends, alive and waiting.

And she'd win the game.

She felt her pocket vibrating and remembered the compass. "Hey...uhh...Captain Kimble?" That didn't feel too weird to say. "Do you need this?" She held it up and he turned around.

A smile spread across his face. "My compass!" He plucked it from Benny's hands and kissed it. "Oh, how I've missed you."

"Does it show us which way to go in the cave?" Benny wondered as he pocketed the compass and started walking again.

"No."

Benny and Zara snuck a glance at each other.

"What does it point to? Evelyn's friends who are trapped?" Zara asked.

"Nope."

"Are you going to tell us anything?" Benny asked.

"Not if I can help it. I've made that mistake before."

"You know how to find the island entrance by memory?" Zara pestered him.

"Yes."

"So what's the compass for? Why did it point me in this direction?" Benny wondered.

He groaned some more, sounding like an old man trapped in a young man's body. "Kid, can we just focus on one thing at a time? Step one: let's get to the island already."

They walked in silence then, Kimble leading the way as the tunnel started to curve upward, the air grew warmer, the breeze lighter, and the whispers Benny had heard before grew louder.

Welcome, Everly Benedict! Welcome!

Her thoughts were coming fast and furious. She couldn't wait to tell Mom. To tell Peter. How would she prove to Peter she'd found the island? Did she need to bring him here? Take pictures with her phone? But before she could figure any of that out, the tunnel was widening, and she heard the sound of rushing water before she saw a wall of water in front of them.

The waterfall Evelyn had described in her journal.

"Good thing you're already wet," Kimble said, walking right through the water to the other side, Ryan still slung over his shoulder.

Benny squeezed Zara's hand. Then Benny took a deep breath and together they stepped through the water. When she emerged, she wiped the water from her eyes.

Trees surrounded the waterfall's pool of water. They swayed gently in the breeze, which smelled like honeysuckle and the sea, and the air was warm from the sun. The *sun*, which she hadn't seen in days, shone bright here, not a cloud in the sky.

Evelyn's island. It was real.

And she was here.

"Are you seeing what I'm seeing?" Zara asked, still clutching Benny's hand.

"I think so," Benny said, her smile growing.

She had the sudden urge to scream at the top of her lungs. To possibly burst into tears. They did it! They found the island. Together. She held tight to Zara's hand. She didn't know what to say. She wasn't sure what came next, but she would figure it out. Just like she'd figured out Evelyn's game. *Do you hear that, Evelyn? I'm here. I'm on your island. I found it.*

"Are you two just going to stand there?" Kimble yelled to them as Ryan hung from his shoulder, like a rag doll. "Or are you going to come to the beach? They're probably waiting."

Benny held her breath. *They* were Evelyn's friends. She and Zara started running, following Kimble through the trees, which led to a long sandy beach that looked out on the kind of turquoise water she'd only seen on computer wallpaper. And then she saw five kids running down the beach toward her.

"It's them," Zara said, squeezing Benny's arm. "It has to be them, right?"

"They're alive," Benny said softly. Her heart was beating so loud then, she could hardly take in the sight of the two girls and three boys, who had stopped a few feet from where Captain Kimble was standing. They looked like they were part of a historical reenactment. Benny tried to figure out who was who. The boy, dark-haired and sullen, was Axel, for certain. A boy with hair the color of sand and a warm smile had to be Gilbert, and the two older teens holding hands were obviously Thomas and Laurel. Finally, a girl with bright red cheeks and long curly brown hair stepped forward.

"Everly Benedict?" she asked, her voice barely a whisper.

"Yes," Benny said. She could feel her whole body shaking. ""Are you Aggy?"

The girl nodded, tears springing to her eyes.

"Aggy," Zara repeated, the name getting caught in her throat.

Aggy smiled at Zara then too before turning back to Benny and embracing her tightly. "Welcome to the island, Everly Benedict. We've been waiting for you a very long time."

TWENTY-SEVEN
BENNY
PRESENT DAY

Benny could feel her hands shaking. Aggy, Evelyn's best friend, the one she'd been reading about in Evelyn's journal all this time was standing in front of her. She was alive. She was still thirteen and had been for the last two hundred.

The idea was mind-blowing.

Every step Evelyn had taken to make sure Benny got to this moment had worked.

We did it, Evelyn, Benny thought, getting emotional. *I found Aggy. I'm here.*

"People call me Benny," Benny told her. She noticed her own voice was barely a whisper.

"As in *Ben*?" asked Gil, confused.

Benny just smiled. So much had changed since 1825. She needed to be gentle in how she explained things. "As in *Benedict*. Benny is my nickname."

"And I'm Zara," Zara chimed in. "As in *Zara Dabney*, and I'm—" She looked at Aggy then and paused. "I'll tell you later."

Aggy took Zara's hand and squeezed. "I know who you are."

Zara opened her mouth and closed it again. She snuck a glance at Benny. "Oh-kay. We will just unpack all that later."

"And I'm Captain Kimble," Ansel interrupted, the gruffness in his voice returning as he stepped into the circle. "And you kids have cost me a lot of time and—"

"We know who you are," Gil butted in. "Aggy explained some things about what's going on with this island. But what I want to know is where is Sparrow? I thought for sure she'd be the one who came for us."

"There are some things I still need to explain, Gil," Aggy said, linking her arm through his. "To all of you, but time isn't on our side. The Blood Orange Moon waits for no one."

"That is for sure, kid," Kimble agreed. "We need to move and fast."

"I don't care about the Blood Orange Moon or where Evelyn is?" Axel snapped. He looked at Benny and Zara. "I just want off this island so lead the way. My father must be worried sick about me."

"Our families too," said Thomas. "We should get back and let them know we're alright and then we can talk."

Aggy gave Benny a pointed look.

Benny inhaled sharply, remembering something she'd read in Evelyn's journal. When Evelyn met Kimble for the first time, he seemed confused about the year. He said something about losing time. Could it be Gil and the others didn't know how much time had passed? Was that possible? Aggy had the gift of sight. Maybe however this island worked, she'd kept that knowledge to herself about the time that had passed.

"And may I ask who is the boy asleep on your shoulder, sir?" Laurel piped up, concerned as always for everyone else instead of herself.

Kimble put Ryan down on the sand, where he stirred for a moment and closed his eyes again. "No clue. And I don't care. What I do care about is this treasure. Now all of you kids stop talking over each other and let me talk," he grumbled. "You're going to make my head explode."

Laurel's eyes widened. "Explode?"

Benny bit her lip. This was going to take some explaining. Maybe the best thing to do was get them all off the island, let them take a hot shower and have a good night's sleep and—wait. Did they even know what a hot shower was? How was she going to explain these people to her mother? To Wally? Did she need to tell Peter she'd found more than an island—she'd found Evelyn's friends? Was her word enough proof to win the game? How had she forgotten her camera? Benny's head was spinning. "We can show you the way off the island and then we'll talk," Benny said and turned back the way she'd come down the beach. "If you'd just follow us."

Aggy coughed.

"Yeah, uh, kid? That's not going to work." Kimble pointed to Benny and Zara. "You? Your friend? You can go whenever you want, but them—" He motioned to Aggy and the others. "They're not going anywhere."

"Why not?" Zara demanded. "They have waited a long time for Benny to break this curse."

"That's what I'm trying to tell you!" Kimble groused. "Everly Benedict didn't break the curse." He looked at Benny. "I'm not saying you can't, but nothing has changed. *Yet.* The curse is very much still alive. And none of us"—he motioned to Aggy and her friends again—"are going to be free till we find it and return the treasure to its original resting place."

"Find what?" Gil demanded.

"The missing piece of treasure!" Kimble said, exasperated. "Evelyn found it, and she wouldn't tell me where it was."

"She did?" Benny did a double-take. "She didn't mention that in her letters or the journal. Are you sure?"

"Of course I'm sure." Kimble looked affronted. "She told me. On more than one occasion over the years." He looked out over the water. "Was quite smug about it too."

"Are you saying we can't leave the island?" Thomas sounded panicked. "We have to go home."

"My father will have your head for this! And Evelyn's," Axel yelled over him, lunging at Kimble, who held him back (he was way bigger obviously). Everyone was shouting now and Benny felt the tension escalate fast.

"Hey, you are more than welcome to leave this island, but guess what?" Kimble shouted. "You're still cursed. You will never age. You will never be able to leave the area around Greenport. So if you want to break the curse, you need to help me find the treasure or we're all doomed to do this for another two hundred years till the next Blood Orange Moon."

"What do you mean we won't age?" Gil demanded now. "You are not making sense."

"If you've done something to us," Axel threatened Kimble, "my father will see to it you are done away with."

"Everyone calm down," Benny jumped in and looked at

everyone. "If there is treasure still to be found, we can find it together, right?"

"There is no treasure on this island, girl!" Axel roared. "If there was, I would have found it."

"Don't talk to her like that!" Gil shouted back.

Zara looked at Benny while the boys argued. "Evelyn wouldn't have left the game half done, would she? Does this mean you didn't win? What is going on here?"

"I don't know." Benny felt ill. Had she missed something? A clue? A riddle? Why wouldn't Evelyn have mentioned there was more treasure out there they needed? How was she supposed to save everyone if the treasure was missing?

Benny felt someone grab her leg. She looked down. Ryan stirred and sat up, looking at them all in confusion. "Where are we?" he asked before his eyes widened. "Are we on the island? Are you all...? Is this real?" he asked before his eyes rolled back and he passed out again.

Kimble whistled loudly. "Everyone quiet! I can't think!"

"Kimble is right," Aggy told the group. "It's going to take all of us working together to figure out how to find the missing treasure so we can all be free."

There was a meow and everyone looked down.

"Winks!" Aggy exclaimed, picking up the cat. "You're back again."

"How do you know my cat?" Kimble exclaimed.

"He's my cat too," Aggy said calmly. "Clearly there are things about this island you don't understand yet either, pirate. Now, are you going to give Everly—I'm sorry, *Benny*—the letter or do I have to take it from you?"

Benny stiffened. "Letter? There's another letter?" She looked from Aggy to Kimble. "From Evelyn?"

Aggy nodded. "Yes."

Kimble grumbled. "I forgot she said you knew about them."

Benny didn't stop to wonder how Aggy knew about the letters. Her heart started flurrying, so fast she was afraid it would pop out of her chest.

Kimble sighed and pulled a yellowed letter out of his pocket. He handed it to Benny. "Kid, take a breath, okay? Yes, Evelyn wrote you more letters and she left this one with me for safe keeping with loads of instructions on when I was supposed to give it to you."

"What is this about?" Zara demanded.

Kimble ran a hand through his hair and huffed loudly. "Something about another game."

"*Another* game?" Benny asked, her voice jumping with excitement and trepidation.

That meant there was more at stake.

More riddles to decipher.

The game was still going.

Or in overtime. (Or whatever sports people said about long games.)

The point was, she wasn't upset to think there were things she didn't understand. That there was mythology and curses and treasure still to find and learn from. Her work wasn't done yet.

Benny stared at the envelope in her hand and smiled at the familiar handwriting. *Hi Evelyn.*

Everyone crowded round the envelope (everyone but Ryan who was still passed out).

"Go ahead, Benny. Read it." Aggy's smile told Benny she knew what the letter was about.

"What does it say?" Gil asked, and Benny read the words aloud.

"'Everly Benedict,'" Benny read. "'First let me say, I'm sorry I tricked you. The game is far from over. In fact, it's only just begun.'"

Benny and her friends will return in *Cursebreaker*, Isle of Ever Book 2.

ACKNOWLEDGMENTS

Sometimes as writers an idea takes hold that we can't stop thinking about. That was the case with *Isle of Ever*, a story I've been imagining since I was a little girl. The story was bigger and more all-encompassing than anything I'd ever tried before and all I kept thinking was: Am I ready to tell a story like this?

The answer was yes, with the right partner, and Sourcebooks has always been the most incredible publisher when I wanted to create a big story that takes us on a fantastical adventure. I'm so thankful to Sourcebooks and Dominquie Raccah for trusting me to create a new series with them. And I'm forever grateful to my editor Wendy McClure, who heard this pitch and dove right in helping me finesse this story that spans two timelines. (She's also an incredible help when it comes to rhyming riddles.)

If you're holding *Isle of Ever* in your hands right now, that's got everything to do with the amazing Sourcebooks team including Shara Zaval, Heather Moore, Sean Murray, Margaret Coffee, Valerie Pierce, and Aimee Alker, Susan Barnett, Chelsey Moler Ford, and Nick Sweeney, who had the herculean feat of keeping everything in this story straight.

I'm so in love with this book cover and design that I have no words to describe them. Thank you, Jessica Nordskog, for making this book so interactive. From the maps to the advertising ads, I'm in awe of how you made this book come alive. Miriam Schwardt, you've spoiled me with a cover illustration more beautiful than anything I could dream up.

To my agent, Dan Mandel, I love how I can throw a wild idea at you and you jump right in helping me make this vision happen. I couldn't ask for a better partner on this publishing journey. Sorry it always feels like we're juggling ten balls in the air at the same time. You make it look easy!

I couldn't have written this book without Alyson Gerber and Mari Mancusi who were subjected to more texts than I should admit where I'd say, "does this scene make sense?" To James Ponti, for reminding me that the opening of *Raiders of the Lost Ark* is a perfect scene and for helping work through all my thoughts on the magic of the island. To Stuart Gibbs, Melissa de la Cruz, and Chris Grabenstein, for the early reads and feedback—I'm incredibly lucky to have such wonderful author friends. And to Christina Diaz Gonzalez for all the legalese regarding Benny's fantastical inheritance—thank you for talking me through it. Any mistakes in this story are mine and mine alone!

I don't like to brag, but I will all day long about Gianna Calonita. Not only am I lucky enough to call this talented young lady family, she is also an excellent student and lover of books. Thank you, Gianna, for reading an early draft of ISLE that you marked up with notes of your own. I'm so lucky to have an editor in my own family!

While this story is clearly fiction, I did take inspiration from many of the towns that made up my childhood summers including Mattituck, Southhold, Jamesport and Greenport. I'm thankful to the East End Seaport Museum for inspiring me and for their incredible Bug Lighthouse Cruise tour that I took last summer. I also learned so much from the lighthouse volunteer at Horton Point who talked to me about working the lighthouse during storms. And to my parents, Nick and Lynn Calonita, Mattituck lifers who called and emailed me every time they found a magazine or article clipping about the north fork in the 1800s. I have most of my research because of you.

Finally, to my family—my husband Mike and two boys, Tyler and Dylan—I know it feels like I've been on deadline for a year, and that's probably because I have been. Thank you for putting up with my piles of research in the dining room, the ring light camera set up when I'm trying to do a post online and for always helping me film things (And figure out filters. And music. Please remember: It's all about angles!) I love all you more than words can say.

Photo: Kimberly L. Photography

ABOUT THE AUTHOR

Jen Calonita is a *New York Times* bestselling author of Twisted Tale novels and the award-winning author of the Royal Academy Rebels and Fairy Tale Reform School series. She spent her childhood summers on the east end of Long Island at her grandparents' house, where she searched for buried treasure. A wannabe mermaid, she lives on land in New York with her husband, two sons, and a feisty Chihuahua named Ben Kenobi. Visit her on the web at jencalonitaonline.com.